BUSTIN' LOOSE

"Keep your head down, Lonaker!" a voice hissed outside his barred jailhouse window.

Lonaker lunged for the cell door. A volley of gun-fire, crackling like heat lightning in the street, mingled with the shattering of window glass and the deadly thud of lead slugs against the timber wall separating the two rooms of the jailhouse.

Crouching, Lonaker watched the sheriff stagger into sight, then sag against the door frame. His pistol slipped from his twitching fingers, then a bullet struck him in the back, hurling him forward in front of the cellblock.

Three hooded men busted through the door. One stood over the moaning lawman, ripped the keys from his belt and threw them at Lonaker, then aimed his .44 at the star-packer's head.

"Make it quick, son," the leader ordered. "We got to ride!"

SHOWDOWN
AT SEVEN SPRINGS

JASON MANNING

ZEBRA BOOKS
KENSINGTON PUBLISHING CORP.

ZEBRA BOOKS

are published by

Kensington Publishing Corp.
475 Park Avenue South
New York, NY 10016

First Printing: December, 1992

Printed in the United States of America

Chapter One

"Stage comin'."

Alkali Jim Sullivan was stretched out in the dust at the crest of the hogback ridge, his head resting on a flat rock and his hat pulled down over his face. When the lookout called, he got to his feet with surprising agility for a big man.

His hair and chin whiskers were sandy red, and his eyes the pale blue of an Arizona sky bleached by the blistering sun. A quid of Lobo Negro bulged his cheek. He spat a stream of brown tobacco juice and flashed a yellow grin.

"Time to strike a blow for the Confederacy, boys."

Pike Slankard and Angel Trinidad roused themselves and forsook the scant shade of a gambel oak, checking their pistols with the methodical attention to detail which a working man gives the tools of his trade.

Slankard was a gaunt, middle-aged man with a salt-and-pepper beard and the eyes of a weasel. His sour expression perfectly reflected his disposition. Trinidad was a stocky half-breed widely acclaimed as one of the ugliest bastards on the Bloody Border. In addition to his pistols, Slankard carried a sawed-off Greener on a shoulder strap. Trinidad's weapons of preference were two big knives, one carried in a boot sheath, the other stuck in his belt.

"Confederacy be damned," growled Slankard. "I'm in this for the money, and so are you, Alkali. How much you reckon our share of this haul will be?"

As he posed this question, Slankard broke open the scattergun to confirm that both barrels were loaded. An ex-sodbuster embittered by life's hardships, he had found the owlhoot trail more to his liking than the endless, back-breaking labor of a hardscrabble farmer.

"I done told you," snapped Alkali Jim. "There'll be a payroll for the bluebellies at Fort Yuma."

"Cain't hardly believe they'd move a payroll without a guard detail to watch over it."

"They don't want to advertise. It's supposed to be a secret."

"I've been wonderin'—who's this inside man who lets you in on all these secrets, Alkali?"

"You're better off not knowing," said Sullivan, steely-eyed.

"You figure?"

"I do. 'Cause if you knew, you might entertain a notion to take over this outfit. And then I'd have to kill you."

Slankard snapped the scattergun closed and gave Alkali Jim a long look. But not too long. Sullivan was the big augur in this pack of two-legged wolves, and Slankard didn't have enough backbone to challenge him.

"Mebbe woman," grinned Trinidad, whose grasp of the English language was tenuous. The loot was of secondary importance to the breed. He enjoyed having his rough way with the ladies, and sometimes carved his name in their soft flesh with his sharp knives, just so they'd have something to remember him by if by some miracle they survived his sadistic attention.

Alkali Jim turned away from the glitter of anticipation in Trinidad's cruel eyes. He didn't much care for the breed's company. Or Slankard's, for that matter. But in this business one didn't get a chance to hobnob with too many gentlemen.

He joined the lookout on the rim of the ridge. The fourth member of the gang was a fuzzy-cheeked younker who wore his matched set of Colt's strapped low on narrow shanks. He called himself the Reno Kid.

"There it is," said the Kid, his voice pitched higher than normal with nervous excitement, pointing at the plume of dun-colored dust in the canyon below.

"I got eyes," said Alkali Jim.

Coyote Canyon was a ribbon of green curling through the arid desert south and west of the Maricopas, a hostile malpais of red sandstone buttes and white alkali flats. Palo verde and tamarisk grew along a rocky wash where weak sweet-water springs maintained small pools of water. A road followed the wash, and it was on this road that Alkali Jim and his highwaymen made their livings. It was the Oxbow Route of the Overland Mail Company.

Sullivan had been preying on the Overland stages for more than a year now. He was confident that this one had a strongbox filled with Yankee money. His informant in the Overland Mail Company had never steered him wrong. Like Sullivan, this inside man was a member of a secret organization called the Knights of the Golden Circle — a brotherhood of Southern sympathizers, thousands strong, dedicated to the proposition that the prosperous state of California would become part of the fledgling Confederate States of America.

Of course, Pike Slankard was right — it was profit, not patriotism, that motivated Alkali Jim. He had to donate most of the Army payroll to the coffers of the Knights. That was part of the deal. So he found himself hoping for a mail pouch on this run, or a couple of well-to-do passengers.

Now he saw the stage, coming up out of a low place sheltered by trees. He let out a low whistle.

"I'll be damned. That ain't no run-of-the-mill mud-wagon like we see most of the time, Kid. That's an honest-to-God Concord coach."

One disgruntled passenger of the Oxbow had called this road the "worst God ever made," and most of the stages were mule-drawn "celerity wagons" built for rough passage, with scant attention paid to the comfort of those poor souls who rode in them.

In spite of its accommodations, the Overland did not want for customers. Though it had been said that the line went "from no place through nothing to nowhere," it was the only transcontinental connection available in 1861 that linked California with the East.

"Let's go," growled Sullivan.

The four men headed for their horses, mounted up. The serpentine canyon curled around the ridge, and they planned to waylay the stage on the opposite side. Down the western slope rode the four, single file, with Sullivan in the lead, down through rocks and cactus and treacherous clumps of wait-a-minute.

As usual, Alkali Jim had selected the ambush spot with the practiced eye of an old hand at the game. Rock outcroppings on either side of the road provided excellent cover. The stage driver wouldn't see them until it was too late.

Sullivan and the breed took one side, Slankard and the Kid the other. All but Slankard drew pistols; Pike unsung the scattergun and rested it on a bony shoulder, ready to bring it sweeping down into action. His assignment was to kill one of the horses if the reinsman tried to whip up the team and make a getaway.

They pulled bandannas up over their faces and waited, grim and silent. The sounds of the stage grew louder as it came around the point of the ridge—the rattle of trace chains, the drumroll of horses cantering at road gait, the creak of the coach as it rocked in its thoroughbraces.

Sullivan timed it perfectly, gadding his horse into the road just as the stage pulled between the rock outcroppings. The leaders of the six-horse-hitch snorted and reared in the traces. Alkali Jim was almost close enough to reach out and touch them. But he spared the antics of the spooked leaders no heed. His cold, unblinking gaze was fixed on the man in the Concord's box. So was the barrel of his charcoal-burner.

"Try bein' a hero and I'll blow daylight through you!" he roared. "Hand over that Army payroll."

With the aplomb of a master, the jehu worked the leathers threaded through his blunt fingers. Checking

9

the swingers and wheelers, he gave the leader lines plenty of play, to prevent the front two horses from fouling the harness.

He was a big man, this reinsman, bigger even than Alkali Jim. He wore a leather vest without a shirt, and his muscle-bound arms were as big around as cannon barrels. Powerful thigh and calf muscles threatened the double-stitched seams of pants made of durable cavalry twill. Sullivan noted that the man did not appear to be "heeled." No gunbelt, no shotgun. Just a bullwhip, twenty feet of braided rawhide coiled like a snake on the seat beside him.

Sullivan noticed something else. The driver didn't seem to be the least bit afraid. Perturbed, but not afraid. A scowl darkened his craggy, square-jawed face—a face so ugly only a mother could love. Compared to this man, Angel Trinidad was handsome. As the other three members of the holdup crew broke cover, the reinsman looked them over with disdain.

Guiding his horse past the six-horse-hitch, Sullivan felt his Irish temper slip its leash. The driver's composure aggravated him. By God, people were supposed to be afraid of four rough characters with faces covered and pistols drawn. This idiot didn't realize how close he was to crossing the river.

As Sullivan came down the left side of the hitch, the Kid did likewise on the offside. The jehu looked from one to the other as he might watch a pair of pesky mosquitoes.

"This is a stickup," growled Sullivan, with a menacing brandish of his pistol.

"I'm not blind," sighed the driver.

"You've got hair on your brisket," begrudged Alkali Jim. "I've always said it's best to kill a brave man quick."

" 'Cowards die many times before their deaths,' " quoted the reinsman. "Shakespeare."

"I'll shoot a few holes in him," offered the Reno Kid. "Let some of that sand out."

"I wouldn't, if I were you," came a voice from inside the coach.

Sullivan swung his pistol around as the coach door on his side opened.

The man who stepped out into the dust of the Coyote Canyon road was tall and slender. He moved with a lithe grace. His eyes were gray and cold, like river ice. He wore a black broadcloth coat and trousers, black boots and hat and string tie. His muslin shirt was white. So were the ivory handles on the matched set of .44 Colt Dragoons carried in crossdraw holsters.

"Who the hell are you?" rasped Sullivan.

"Name's Lonaker."

Alkali Jim no longer felt the heat of the summer sun.

"I've heard of you."

"Then you know I'm the law on this road. You're under arrest."

Sullivan barked an ugly laugh. "That's bold talk."

Lonaker smiled.

"I can back it up."

Chapter Two

All four road agents had heard of John Clayton Lonaker. Few outlaws in the Territory were unacquainted with Lonaker's reputation. Fewer still had any desire whatsoever to become acquainted with the man behind the legend. Most who had done so were either dead or behind bars.

So Alkali Jim Sullivan and his three colleagues in crime stopped thinking about a successful holdup and started worrying about just staying alive as soon as Lonaker stepped out of the Concord.

John Lonaker wasn't a badge-toter, but he was the law on the Oxbow Route. He was the Overland Mail Company's troubleshooter. Rumor had it he stayed on the road day and night, always on the move. You never knew where he might show up, or when. He lived in a custom Concord, built to his specifications by the New Hampshire firm of Abbot & Downing. He answered to no one except Henry Wells and William Fargo, the two visionary entrepreneurs who had recently bought the Overland from its bankrupt founder, John Butterfield. Every person on the Overland payroll did what Lonaker told them to do, or found themselves out of a job. That applied to division agents as well as lowly hostlers.

Sullivan cursed himself for a dunderpated fool. His informer had told him only that an Army payroll would be rolling through Coyote Canyon at about midday, without a guard detail. He realized now that the appearance of the Concord, when a celerity wagon was expected, should have forewarned him. Greed had blinded him. And hindsight was as worthless as a four-card flush.

Was it mere coincidence that Lonaker had been passing through Coyote Canyon this day and sprung the trap? Or had the Overland troubleshooter known about the plan to steal the Army payroll? If the latter were true, then either the inside man had been found out, or he'd pulled a double cross. Alkali Jim always expected the worst. That way, he was seldom disappointed.

"You're in the wrong place at the wrong time, Lonaker," sneered Sullivan. This seemed like a good time for bravado.

"I don't think so," replied Lonaker. He was calm, cordial. Not a trace of hostility. But Alkali Jim wasn't fooled. Lonaker was a coldhearted killer. He had no fear, gave no quarter. He was a fast draw, quick to kill. Sullivan felt only marginally better for having his pistol drawn and aimed at the troubleshooter.

"You're going to die, Lonaker," he growled, finger tightening on trigger.

Lonaker nodded. "Someday. But not by your hand, Sullivan."

"How did . . . ?"

"I know. That must be Pike Slankard back there with the scattergun. And Angel Trinidad with the belduques." Gray eyes flicked to the Reno Kid. "This one is new to me."

"I'm the Reno Kid." The gun-hung youngster talked fast and high. "And after today everybody'll know who I am — the man who killed John Lonaker hisself."

Although positioned on the other side of the team from the troubleshooter, the Kid had a fairly clear shot at Lonaker's upper body. He fired both Colts. But Lonaker moved a fraction of a second before the Kid started making smoke. Alkali Jim had never seen a man move so fast. In the blink of an eye Lonaker was diving beneath the Concord. When he rolled out on the other side, the colt Dragoons were drawn.

The Reno Kid got off two more shots. One bullet kicked up road dust. The other carved a long groove in the Concord's bodywork. On his belly, elbows firmly planted, Lonaker returned fire. Both slugs struck the Kid in the chest, lifting him out of the saddle. He flopped backward and slipped off the croup of his horse, dead before he hit the ground.

Flinching away from all this gunplay, the Kid's horse trampled the corpse of its erstwhile owner in its haste to make tracks. The passage between the rock outcroppings was narrow, and the panicky mount collided with Slankard's pony on its way out. This affected Pike's aim just as Slankard triggered one barrel of the sawed-off. Double-ought buckshot

14

peppered the left side of the driver's box—nowhere near the reinsman, who was leaping to the right.

Two hundred pounds and then some of muscle, bone and pure grit hurtled through the air and carried Alkali Jim clean out of his center-fire rig. Sullivan took the brunt of the fall. It was a testament to his toughness that he took it and kept on fighting. He tried to split the jehu's skull open with his pistol. The driver blocked the blow with his left arm. Sullivan noticed his adversary was holding the coiled bullwhip in that hand.

This was the last thing Alkali Jim noticed. The driver's huge fist slammed into his face right between the eyes, crushing the cartilage in his nose. Sullivan saw a flash of blinding light and passed out.

Cursing a blue streak, Pike Slankard fired his second load of buckshot at Lonaker. He missed. Lonaker had rolled back under the coach, anticipating just such a reaction from the ex-sodbuster-turned-outlaw.

Gun thunder rolled down the canyon. The team surged in their traces, no longer constrained by the reinsman. The stagecoach lurched forward.

"Gotcha, you sonuvabitch!" exulted Slankard, tossing the empty scattergun aside and yanking a pistol out of his belt with one hand while savagely neck-reining his prancing mount with the other.

He expected a clear shot at Lonaker once the team had pulled the coach forward.

But as the Concord rolled by him, all Pike saw was empty road.

Slankard had a handful of seconds to be perplexed. Then Lonaker let go of the rear axle cross-brace. Flat on his back, he fired straight up into Slankard. The Colt Dragoons spat flame and death. Lonaker rolled away from the hooves of the longrider's horse.

Slankard pitched sideways off his mount. One of the bullets shattered his jaw and blew the top of his head off. His horse leaped like a jackrabbit and took off at a gallop. Slankard's foot twisted in the stirrup, and the horse dragged his mortal remains up-canyon.

Seeing his three *compañeros* dealt with so summarily, Angel Trinidad decided discretion was the better part of valor. He savagely reined his horse around and dug deep with big-roweled Chihuahua spurs. Bent low in the saddle, he sent a couple of shots in the general direction of Lonaker and the reinsman. He wasn't aiming, and didn't hit anything but real estate.

Straddling Alkali Jim's unconscious form, the stage driver unlimbered the bullwhip with a sharp wrist action and let fly. Angel's mustang was still in its first full stride when braided rawhide twined around the outlaw's arm. Huck held onto the whip's three-foot hickory handle and braced himself. Trinidad suddenly found himself suspended in midair, his horse running right out from under him. He hit the ground, bounced up, discovered that he'd lost his pistol, and reached for the knife in his belt.

The reinsman gave the whip a hard pull. The breed pitched forward into the dirt. With another practiced flick of the wrist, the driver freed the whip and closed in. Angel came up on one knee and lashed

16

out with the knife. Eluding this vicious stroke, the reinsman clubbed Trinidad with the whip handle. Angel sprawled, scrambled to his feet, and blinked blood out of his eyes. With a wolfish snarl, he lunged, his blade flashing hot sunlight.

A gun spoke.

Trinidad seemed to run headlong into an invisible stone wall. A blue hole had suddenly appeared in his forehead. A look of astonishment frozen by death on his swarthy features, the breed toppled like a cut tree.

The reinsman glanced over his shoulder at Lonaker, who was strolling forward through a motionless haze of pale yellow dust. One Colt Dragoon was back in its holster. Lonaker was methodically reloading the other.

"You never learn, Huck," he admonished gently. "Once you knock 'em down, make sure they're down forever."

"I don't have the stomach for killing that you do, Mr. Lonaker."

Reproach put a sharp edge to the reinsman's words. Lonaker smiled faintly.

"How long have we worked together?"

"A long time."

Lonaker nodded. "But I never can seem to come to terms with the fact that you have a gentle spirit. Maybe it's because I saw you pound so many men into bloody pulp during your career as a prizefighter."

"I'm not proud of that."

Lonaker gazed down at the dead half-breed with

stony impassivity. The reinsman watched Lonaker. It was funny, mused Huck Odom. He'd worked for Lonaker going on three years, and neither one understood the other. They'd been in many scrapes together, but Huck still couldn't decide whether the Overland troubleshooter was one of the finest men he'd ever met, or one of the worst.

A vein of cold ruthlessness ran deep in Lonaker. Most of the time it was well-hidden behind a polite, soft-spoken, reserved facade. But when it came down to kill-or-be-killed, John Clayton Lonaker became a passionless dealer of death. Most men in peril just tried to stay alive. Lonaker became a machine, fearless and merciless. In such moments, even Huck was afraid of him.

The reinsman figured it had a lot to do with Laura. He'd not had the privilege of knowing Lonaker's wife. She'd died prior to Huck's quitting the ring and coming to work for the Overland. People said something in Lonaker had died, too, the day they laid Laura to final rest.

They whispered that John Lonaker had no soul.

Watching the troubleshooter now, Huck Odom almost believed it.

Chapter Three

They put leg irons and manacles on Alkali Jim Sullivan, still sprawled senseless in the road. The team had not taken the coach far. Lonaker got Sullivan draped over a shoulder and carried the outlaw to the Concord. Huck clambered into the box, and Lonaker handed Alkali Jim up to him.

Of only average height and build, the Overland troubleshooter nonetheless possessed extraordinary strength — a fact demonstrated by the ease with which he handled Sullivan, who was certainly no bantam weight.

Huck deposited the unconscious road agent on the top rack. Stout leather straps were fixed to the railing, and the burly reinsman squaw-hitched these to the irons decorating Sullivan's wrists and ankles, so that Alkali Jim couldn't roll off the Concord, accidentally or otherwise.

"What about the others?" asked Huck.

"What about them?"

Huck looked meaningfully up at the blistered sky. The first turkey vulture was already circling.

In response, Lonaker fished an Ingersoll key-winder out of a coat pocket, and just as meaningfully consulted it.

"McGrath and the others will be waiting on us at Lime Creek. I don't like to be late."

Huck smirked. "If we had all day we still wouldn't, would we?"

"You know how I feel about it."

Huck nodded. "I know. Buzzards get hungry, too. You're a hard man, Mr. Lonaker."

Lonaker pulled a small book, bound in black leather, out of his coat's inside breast pocket. As he walked back up the Coyote Canyon road, he thumbed through the pages. Each page was a wanted poster in miniature, complete with sketch, name and aliases if any, descriptions including any distinguishing marks and habits, a list of preferred weapons, and a history of past crimes.

This Lonaker called his "bible." In it were catalogued over eighty outlaws who had been or still were known to be operating in Texas, the Territory and southern California—the range of the two-thousand-mile Oxbow Route. Texas Rangers were said to carry a similar compendium, which they referred to as a Book of Wanted Men.

Sitting on his heels beside the body of Angel Trinidad, Lonaker compared the breed's features with a sketch in his bible, just to make sure. He nodded to himself, tore the page out, and stuffed it under Trinidad's shirt. He went next to Pike Slankard, whose carcass had been dragged some distance up the road by his runaway horse. Pike's bandanna-mask was still in place. Lonaker removed it. Another page was torn from the book and left on the body. Flies were already wallowing in the terrible, gaping wound at the top of Slankard's skull. Lonaker freed Pike's boot from the stirrup and led the horse back to the stagecoach.

The troubleshooter had logged many hours studying his Book of Wanted Men. He'd been pretty sure about the identities of the masked robbers from the start. All except the Reno Kid. He didn't bother checking the youngster against his bible. The Kid hadn't lived long enough to earn a page in John Lonaker's black book.

Catching up the Kid's cayuse, and Sullivan's, he hitched the horses to the back of the Concord with Pike's mount. Trinidad's horse was long gone.

Huck was carefully extracting buckshot pellets out of the coach with a clasp knife, scowling as he worked.

"How many?" asked Lonaker.

"Six," was Huck's cross reply. "This isn't so bad, but she's got a nasty bullet groove on the off side. You know how many that makes?"

"Tell me," said Lonaker tolerantly.

"One hundred and twelve." Huck sounded thoroughly disgusted. Every scratch, dent and bullethole the Concord suffered severely vexed him. The red-painted coach, with its gracefully cambered sides, its black leather front and rear, and its gold-painted undercarriage and wheels, was Huck's pride and joy. He had christened her Betsy, and treated her like a lady.

"You can plug them up and paint them over later," said Lonaker, climbing into the coach. "Let's roll. We should make Lime Creek station in an hour."

"Sure. If we sprout wings and fly." Huck settled in the driver's box and threaded the leathers through fingers that were like agile steel. " 'In wicked haste is no profit,' " he muttered to the unconscious Alkali Jim laid out on the top rack behind him. "Chaucer."

He flicked harness with a lusty geehaw and made a fast, smooth pullout.

Lonaker heard every word. He shook his head. Huck Odom was a strange one. Educated at Harvard, groomed by his family to become a lawyer, Huck instead had struck out for a life of adventure. He'd been an expressman in New England, learning the "Yankee style" of reinsmanship. Then he'd sailed around the Horn on a clipper ship. Then he'd taken up prizefighting in California. And now he was the aide, driver and conscience of the Overland Mail's troubleshooter.

While ordinary Concords boasted three interior benches and were capable of carrying nine passengers, Lonaker's custom-built coach had only one upholstered bench, located forward, just behind the front boot. Sitting there, Lonaker let his gaze wander idly over the interior of his home on wheels.

Opposite him was a cabinet with numerous

22

locked drawers, a map case, and a sliding leaf which, when pulled out, became a writing desk. Above the cabinet were two small shelves laden with books held in place by small brass rails that could be swung down out of the way when a book was needed.

Alongside the cabinet was a glass-fronted guncase which held two rifles and a shotgun. The latter was a ten-gauge Remington with twenty-eight-inch barrels. One of the rifles was the brand new Henry .44—the first practical lever-action repeater. It held fifteen rimfire shells in a tubular magazine. The other long gun was a Sharps-Borschardt .45, the powerful "buffalo gun," with an effective range of over a mile.

The bottom part of the guncase contained large quantities of ammunition for these weapons, and the Colt Dragoons which the Overland troubleshooter favored. An assortment of other guns were carried in a velvet-lined drawer: a Barns .50 caliber boot pistol, a Remington .41 over-and-under derringer, and a Whitney .38 hideout.

The bench itself was another compartment with a hinged top, in which Lonaker kept clothes, blankets, foodstuffs, water, and several bottles of Tennessee sour mash and imported brandy.

Two interior lamps and a large silver chronometer were secured to the walls. There was a hatch in the roof and another in the floor. A small sliding panel above Lonaker's head allowed him to communicate with Huck in the driver's box without having to lean out one of the windows.

The coachmakers, Abbot and Downing, were recognized masters of their craft. Every Concord was a work of art, unequaled for speed, comfort and durability. "It don't break down—it only wears out," was the unanimous endorsement of expressmen across the country.

Lonaker's coach was sturdier than most. The side panels of seasoned basswood had been reinforced with a second layer of hickory, making the coach virtually bullet-proof. In addition to leather window flaps, hickory shutters complete with crosscut gun slots had been added. The iron-rimmed wheels and the undercarriage had been strengthened with additional ironwork. Two extra wheels were carried in the rear boot, along with Lonaker's rimfire saddle. The front boot was deeper than most, with hickory panels behind the black leather casing. Huck could slip off the box and down into the boot and be fairly well protected from bullets, arrows and similar mischief.

All in all, Lonaker was satisfied with the coach. It had served him well over the years. He wasn't as attached to it as Huck seemed to be—but then he'd disciplined himself not to become attached to anything. Or anyone.

Taking a cheroot from a box in one of the cabinet drawers, he flicked a sulphur match to flame with his thumbnail and lighted up. Settling back on the upholstered seat, he propped one booted foot on the small ironbound chest which contained the payroll for the Fort Yuma garrison.

Hand over that Army payroll.

How had Alkali Jim Sullivan known?

It was quite by chance that Lonaker had the payroll in his possession. They had passed the regular stage, broken down by the wayside, two hours back in the direction of Gila Bend. Lonaker's decision to take the chest on at least as far as the Lime Creek station had been spur-of-the-moment. The money was safer in his keeping.

Obviously, Sullivan had been expecting the regular stage which, had it not been delayed, would have passed through Coyote Canyon about now. The only way he could have known about the Army payroll was by dent of inside information. The payroll was a great temptation to the many outlaws plaguing the Oxbow Route, not to mention the host of bandits lurking just south of the border. Its transport had been a well-kept secret — or so Lonaker had thought.

Maybe, he mused, it was a good thing Huck Odom had a healthy aversion to killing. Alkali Jim was alive. Dead men couldn't talk.

Lonaker made exposing the inside man his first priority. Whoever the informer was, he was pretending to serve the best interests of the Overland. Men like Sullivan were bad enough, but at least they made no bones about who and what they were. Lonaker could not abide traitors.

The inside man was going to answer to him.

Chapter Four

Like so many stations along the Oxbow Route, Lime Creek was an adobe structure with a sod roof. Squat and homely, it stood backed up against the base of a butte, facing a sagebrush flat spotted with saguaro. Nearby, a spring bubbled out of a crevice in the rock, trickling water into a stony draw. A few scrawny ironwood trees offered scant shade for livestock kept in a rock-walled corral.

Lime Creek was a "home" station, and hence was larger than most, providing lay-over accommodations for drivers and passengers. It was operated by a man named Jute Venard and his wife Emily. Jute was a spry old gristleneck with horse-warped legs and a sunny disposition. It was hard not to like Jute.

The same could not be said for his wife. Emily Venard was a stern, lugubrious woman who never smiled and seldom spoke. The drivers had a nickname for her: Ol' Stoneface. The Venards were living proof that opposites did indeed attract.

Jute and the station's hostler came out to greet

Lonaker and Huck as the latter climbed the reins and brought Betsy to a halt in front of the station.

"That there's a poor way to treat a passenger on the Overland, Mr. Lonaker," joked Venard, squinting up at Alkali Jim on the top rack. Sullivan had regained consciousness. He glowered at Lonaker and the station agent.

"In life, you get what you deserve," replied the troubleshooter. "Jute, meet Jim Sullivan."

"Alkali Jim?"

"The same. Got a safe place to keep him?"

Jute tilted a sweat-stained slouch hat forward over his eyes and scratched the back of his head.

"The smokehouse will do," he decided. "Built to keep varmints out, so I reckon it'll keep one in."

Huck removed the leather straps from Sullivan's leg-irons and manacles. Alkali Jim sat up slowly. His face was badly swollen around the nose and eyes, puffy and purple-streaked.

"You pack a punch," he mumbled to Huck.

"You're just lucky," said Huck.

"Funny. I don't feel lucky." The outlaw's words were muffled, as though he were talking through a mouthful of cotton. His mustache was caked with dried blood.

"Well, you are. You're lucky you had me to deal with, and not him." Huck nodded at Lonaker.

Sullivan gave Lonaker a long appraisal. "Shoulda gunned you down first thing."

"You were talking when you should have been shooting," concurred Lonaker. "Now get down."

The outlaw grabbed hold of the top rack railing, rolled his body over the side, and lowered himself to the ground. It was no easy matter for a shackled man, but he asked for no help, and no one offered any.

"Watch you don't scratch the paint," rebuked Huck.

"Seen the westbound run?" Jute asked Lonaker.

"It'll be along."

"How'd you meet up with this character?"

"He and his gang were laying up for the regular stage in Coyote Canyon."

"What happened to the rest of the gang? Get away?"

"Buzzard bait," said Huck.

Three men emerged from the station in time to hear this exchange. Lonaker knew them — McGrath, Coffman and Raney. All three were Overland division agents.

Sid McGrath was a brawny man with a square, gray-freckled face, thinning black hair, and eyes as hard and cloudy as agate. Phil Coffman was a tall, thin, taciturn Texan, as soft-spoken as McGrath was blustery. Homer Raney was a small, round-shouldered individual with the doleful features of a bloodhound.

The trio were distinctly different from one another in appearance. Yet in one important respect they were quite similar. Each in his own way effectively handled the monumental responsibilities of overseeing a division on the Overland.

"Alkali Jim Sullivan," said McGrath sourly. "Yonder's a tree. Now, if we can lay hand on a rope . . ."

Lonaker shook his head. "No lynching, Sid."

"You call it lynching?" boomed the leather-lunged McGrath. "I say it's justice."

That was McGrath—blunt and brutal, a man who cut no slack for anyone, least of all himself.

"I'll take him on to Yuma," said Lonaker. "Turn him over to the territorial marshal. How about that smokehouse, Jute?"

"Follow me," said Venard.

He started off around the station. Sullivan shuffled behind him, and Lonaker followed the outlaw. The three division agents brought up the rear, interested observers. The hostler, a man Lonaker didn't know, began to unhitch the lathered team. Lonaker relied on Huck to watch over the payroll. Huck always kept his wits about him. He wasn't the kind who needed telling.

The smokehouse was unlike any Lonaker had seen. A shallow cave had been closed up with a wall of perfectly joined rocks. A timbered door reinforced with strap iron was set into the man-made wall. The door was padlocked on the outside. Jute carried the key with him. The interior, roughly twelve feet square, was dark and cool. A big fire-pit had been hollowed out of the stone floor, a circle of cold black ash inches deep. Iron hooks had been hammered into the ceiling. Part of a dressed out beef hung from one of these. A couple of kegs and a crate filled with airtights stood in one corner.

"Come across a ladino a week ago," said Jute proudly, indicating the beef. "How thick you like your steak, Mr. Lonaker?"

Lonaker smiled but did not answer. He was all business. A quick glance satisfied him that there was no way out of the smokehouse save for the door. The hinges were exterior, and the door fit snugly into the sturdy beams employed as the jambs and header of its frame.

"This will do," he decided.

"Stayed in worse," mumbled Sullivan. "How 'bout a light, boys?"

McGrath, standing just outside, spoke up. "You're not afraid of the dark, are you, Sullivan?"

Lonaker and Venard stepped back outside. The troubleshooter watched while the station agent secured the padlock.

"You look like you got trampled by a herd of wild horses, John," observed Coffman in that quiet way of his. Lonaker's broadcloth coat and trousers were torn in a couple of places and covered with pale dust. His white muslin shirt was no longer white.

"You shouldn't dress so well if you're going to keep getting into scrapes with bandits," added Raney.

"It's a dirty job," joked McGrath.

"I'll change later," said Lonaker. "But first we talk."

Venard said, "I'll leave you gentlemen to cuss

and discuss."

He headed back into the station. Lonaker led the division agents to a ribbon of blue shade against the north wall of the adobe building. The hostler passed out of earshot, leading the team to the corral.

"Who is that?" Lonaker asked McGrath.

Sid McGrath's division included Lime Creek. Raney supervised the stretch between Tucson and Gila Bend. Coffman's division was to the west, from Fort Yuma to San Diego. McGrath's lay between the two. Each man was responsible for the hiring and firing of personnel in their division.

"Goes by the name of Fallon," replied McGrath. "Slim Greaves got the itch to yonder. Just up and disappeared one day, or so Jute tells me. Couple days later Fallon drifted in and Jute put him to work. I okayed it. That's what we get, you know, most of the time, by way of hostlers, and even some of the swing station keepers. Drifters and saddle bums. They might stay a month or a year. You never can tell." McGrath shrugged thick shoulders.

"That's part of what I wanted to talk to you men about," said Lonaker. "First, though, I want to thank you, Phil, for coming this far to meet me."

"That's okay," said Coffman. "I like to have a chance to see how Sid here runs his stretch. Makes me right proud of mine."

McGrath grinned. He fished a half-smoked claro cigar out of his coat pocket and stuck it in his

31

teeth. "Hell, Phil, you couldn't make a profit running a whorehouse, much less a stage line."

Lonaker turned to Raney. "Sorry I missed you in Tucson."

"Not your fault that I was up Maricopa way. Buying some stock off a short line that went belly up. Got your wire there." Raney looked even more somber than usual. "Tell us what happened in Texas, John?"

"Trouble," was Lonaker's grim reply. "We managed to get some of the coaches and stock moved up the line to Lordsburg. But most of our employees in Texas used the secession as an excuse to make off with company property."

Raney heaved a soulful sigh. "My God. This country's coming apart."

"I can't believe Texas has gone with the Confederacy," said Coffman, like a man who has learned his wife has been unfaithful. "I thought Sam Houston could keep her in the Union."

"He did his best," said Lonaker. "But for once his best wasn't good enough."

"So what does this mean for the Overland?" wondered McGrath.

"Wells and Fargo have made it clear to the United States government that the Overland is committed to the Union," said Lonaker. "California is the key, gentlemen. That state must not fall into the hands of the Confederacy. Its wealth would go a long way toward financing the rebellion. As it stands now, the Overland is the only line of communication open between California and the rest of the Union. The Overland still has the U.S. Mail contract, and our bosses have assured the government that the line will stay open, at all cost."

"You can count on me," said McGrath gruffly. "How about you, Phil?"

There was no levity in his tone when he addressed Coffman this time. They were friendly rivals—both men fiercely competing to make their division the best on the Oxbow. But McGrath looked less than friendly now. He eyed the tall Texan with blatant suspicion. Civil war, thought Lonaker, was very uncivil in the way it pitted friend against friend.

"I suppose you have every right to question my loyalty to the Union," said Coffman, despondent. "And to the Overland. If you want my resignation because I come from Texas, John, you can have it."

Lonaker was a good judge of character, and he relied on his instincts. His instincts told him that Phil Coffman was a man of integrity.

"The Oxbow needs every good man it can get. Things are going to get rough from here on in. If you want to follow the course your home state has chosen, then resign, and you have my word we'll part company as friends. Just don't swear allegiance to the Union, and the Overland, and then break your oath. That goes for all of you. For everyone on the line." Lonaker laid a hand on one of his pistols. "Because if a man does that, he'd better start shooting the next time he sees me."

33

Chapter Five

The three division agents knew this was no idle threat. If Lonaker said it, he meant it, and he followed words with action. What the troubleshooter had just issued was a stern warning as well as a solemn promise — and both were as deadly as an Apache knife to the throat.

"Thing is," said Raney, "we have no way of knowing just how many of our employees entertain rebel sentiments."

"I had a notice printed up in Lordsburg," said Lonaker. "The essence of it is what I just relayed to you. The Overland sticks with the Union. Any employee who doesn't find that to his liking needs to draw his pay and dust out. By the time each of you gets back to his office, he'll find a stack of those notices waiting for him. See to it that every employee in your division gets one."

"Fair warning," said McGrath.

"Right. And no man is to be bad-mouthed or laid a hand on if he follows his convictions and declares for the Confederacy."

"Problem is, the slaveholders were the ones who picked the Oxbow Route in the first place," grumbled McGrath, belligerently gnawing on his unlit claro.

Lonaker nodded. The history of the Oxbow was tainted with the stench of politics. Five years ago California had petitioned the United States Congress for a transcontinental stageline. The state felt isolated from the rest of the Union. The traditional sea passage was too slow. And when California spoke, the rest of the nation listened. Its population had swelled to half a million after the gold rush. Its rich mines, abundant timberland and Pacific ports were priceless resources. California was the linchpin of the nation's "manifest destiny."

But California's request had become a sticky issue in a Congress seething with sectional discord. The antislavery faction wanted the stage route to follow already established emigrant trails which moved in a northerly direction from St. Louis. Representatives from the states below the Mason-Dixon line were just as determined to see the link with California take a more southerly route.

Both sides believed the first transcontinental railroad would inevitably follow the route of the first overland stage line, and the slaveholders realized that the location of the railroad would be crucial to their goal of expanding the institution of slavery. Northerners were committed to keeping the frontier untarnished by that "peculiar institution."

As it was wont to do, Congress waffled on the issue, finally agreeing to pay $600,000 a year for semi-weekly mail deliveries by stagecoach between the Mississippi River and the California coast, and delegating the responsibility of selecting the exact route to someone else. That someone else turned out to be the Postmaster General. Unfortunately for the abolitionists, the Postmaster General, Aaron Brown, had been a proslavery man from Tennessee. To the chagrin of the North, the Oxbow Route was chosen, with its eastern terminus in Texas.

"I say we ought to move the whole line further north," added McGrath. "It's a miracle Butterfield ever made the Oxbow work in the first place."

"I agree," seconded Raney. "What's wrong with the route the Pony Express took? St. Joseph, across the plains, through South Pass, skirt the Great Salt Lake, then over the Sierra Nevada to Sacramento."

"Maybe," said Lonaker. "But for now, the U.S. Mail is delivered on the Oxbow. And nothing must stop the U.S. Mail."

"The Knights of the Golden Circle will try," warned Coffman. "They're playing hell in my division. I've heard a rumor that the Confederacy, through the Knights, has made an offer of amnesty to all outlaws once the Southwest becomes Rebel territory. The Knights are bent on shutting us down, and they've got an army of longriders willing to help them do it."

"Hire all the extra guns you need," said Lonaker. "In case you hadn't noticed, gentlemen, we've got a war on our hands."

"Problem is, the Golden Circle is a secret society. I

believe they'll try to infiltrate the Overland, destroy us from within," said Coffman.

"Maybe they've already started. Sullivan knew about the Army payroll bound for Fort Yuma. He knew the day it was scheduled to pass through Coyote Canyon."

The division agents fired looks of alarm between themselves.

The Overland had devised a scheme designed to camouflage shipments of cash and gold. Strongboxes were sent up and down the line on almost every stage. Most of them were weighed down with worthless rock. It was a variation on the old "shell game." It was hoped that this would keep the road agents guessing. Not even the stage drivers and station employees were supposed to know which strongboxes held the payrolls and bullion. The boxes were kept locked, and each was to be handled and guarded as though it contained a king's ransom. Only the division agents—and Lonaker—were privy to the truth.

"I'm not accusing any one of you," said Lonaker.

"Sullivan's inside man might be a station agent somewhere along the line who happens to be handy at picking locks on strongboxes."

His cold gray eyes skimmed across the features of the three men. Clearly, he'd succeeded in impressing them with the gravity of the situation.

"Well, that's all I wanted to say. I've got the payroll. I'll see it safely to Fort Yuma. Just keep your eyes skinned. The Confederacy wants the Overland closed down and California isolated. It's up to us to see that they fail."

"You think Sullivan might tell you who this inside man is?" asked Raney.

"Give me ten minutes alone with him," growled McGrath, smacking fist into hand. "I'll beat it out of him."

Lonaker's smile was remote. He figured Sullivan was too tough a nut for even McGrath to crack. "I'm going to talk to him now."

Turning the corner of the station house, he almost collided with Jute Venard.

"Come to tell you gents that the vittles are ready," reported the station agent. "Mr. McGrath and Mr. Raney best set to table soon, 'cause the eastbound'll be rolling in shortly. And we set a place for you and Huck, Mr. Lonaker."

"Thanks, Jute." The next eastbound stage would take McGrath and Raney back to their respective division headquarters. The former worked out of Gila Bend, the latter from Tucson.

A ribbon of smoke was snaking out of the station's chimney, carrying aromas that ignited the troubleshooter's appetite. But he had business to attend to, and Lonaker always put business before anything else. He borrowed the smokehouse key from Jute and walked on.

Angling across the yellow hardpack toward the smokehouse, he passed Fallon going the other way. The hostler was leading fresh horses to the Concord. He was a man of medium build and nondescript features splotched with blue whisker stubble. Whiskey-colored eyes flicked at Lonaker. He nodded curtly and moved along, whistling a tune. It wasn't "Dixie," noted Lonaker, who turned to watch him go. Fallon didn't glance back or act nervous. The trouble-shooter shrugged and walked on.

This was a different kind of game, mused Lonaker, and he wondered if he was equipped to play it. His was a straightforward nature. He met trouble head-on. There wasn't a deceitful bone in his body. But this business of secret societies and infiltrators was the kind of trouble that slipped up on a person from the blindside. Lonaker realized he might have to do a little sidewinding himself if he was going to win this time.

He took the precaution of stepping to one side as he swung open the smokehouse door. This was a well-advised move. Jim Sullivan hit the door with his shoulder as it began to open. The door cracked back on its iron hinges and Sullivan caromed off at an angle, hopping to keep his balance, a difficult task for a man adorned with leg irons. Lonaker tripped him. The outlaw toppled, cursing. The troubleshooter dragged him back into the smokehouse.

"That was a long chance you just took," said Lonaker. "I might have shot you."

"Better that than going back to that hellhole of a territorial prison," mumbled Sullivan, truculent. "You know I broke out of there once."

"I know."

"Made 'em look bad. They'll take it out on me."

"You're tough. You'll survive."

"They can make your life unfit for living."

"That's where the owlhoot trail leads. That, or Boot Hill. You knew that when you chose to ride it."

"Wasn't a choice, exactly. Just happened."

Lonaker sat on one of the kegs and gave Sullivan a long, curious study. The outlaw's last remark had a wistful quality. All he knew about Sullivan were details of a notorious career of longriding. He knew nothing about the life Sullivan had led prior to turning to banditry. Do-good reformers claimed that men like Alkali Jim were forced into a life of crime by hard luck and society's cold shoulder. Lonaker didn't think he'd ever buy that bill of goods, but he had a notion that there was still a thread of decency left in Sullivan.

"Maybe they'll hang me," said Sullivan, a crooked grin pushing his swollen face around. "I ain't never killed nobody, but I rode with them that did. Pike was a quick trigger. And Angel . . ." Sullivan shook his head. "Christ, that was one mean sonuvabitch. Never dared turn my back on him."

"Who told you about the Army payroll?"

Sullivan's pain-rimmed eyes glittered with cold reproach.

"Wouldn't you like to know."

"Why I asked."

"Well, you can go straight to hell. I ain't never turned anybody in, and I never will."

"Real noble," said Lonaker. "Wonder if he'd do the same for you?"

"I make my own rules, and live by 'em. If I told you, would you let me go?"

"You know I wouldn't."

"I didn't think so."

"But I could speak on your behalf. Make sure the

40

judge knows you cooperated."

"I'll never stand before a judge, Lonaker."

"Think somebody will break you out? The Knights of the Golden Circle, maybe?"

Though Sullivan didn't respond, his expression betrayed him, informing Lonaker that Alkali Jim had some connection with the secessionists.

"Maybe you'll change your mind," said the troubleshooter, standing. He hadn't really expected Sullivan to talk, and in a way he admired the outlaw for not talking. Lonaker put great store in loyalty. Even misplaced loyalty.

He stepped through the doorway into hot afternoon sunlight.

Sullivan said, "It's black and cold as the grave in here, Lonaker. You ever think about dying?"

"Not much."

"I do. I reckon being dead is like being asleep. A long, deep sleep." Sullivan seemed to look right through Lonaker, at something way out yonder that only he could see. "I could use the rest. I'm bone-tired. Been a long time sleeping with one eye open."

Lonaker closed the door, secured the padlock, and walked away.

Chapter Six

By the time Lonaker got back to the Concord, Fallon and Huck had finished hitching up the fresh team. The hostler disappeared into the station. The division agents were also inside. Jute came out to fetch the smokehouse key.

"The missus fixed a plate up for your prisoner, Mr. Lonaker," said Venard. "If that's okay with you."

"Fine. But tell her to be careful. Sullivan's a desperate man. No fork or knife, not even a spoon. He can eat with his hands."

"I'll make sure he don't try nothin'," promised Jute. "You can count on me."

Watching Venard return to the station, Lonaker wondered about that. Yesterday he would have put complete faith in Jute Venard. Now he didn't know who he could trust.

The station agent reappeared in Emily Venard's wake. She carried a plate covered with a scrap of linen to keep flies out of the food. A rawboned woman, twice her husband's size, she wore a drab calico dress and an apron. Her square-jawed face was harsh and humorless. She spared Lonaker a fathomless glance. He knew very little about her. She kept to herself, and was just barely civil to those who visited Lime Creek.

As the Venards rounded the corner of the station, Huck completed his double-check of the hitch and joined Lonaker.

"I know it's not proper to speak unkindly of others," said the reinsman, "but every time I see Emily Venard it makes me glad I never got married. The woman's got a mean eye. I feel sorry for Jute. Can't imagine what he saw in her."

" 'When the candles are out all women are fair,' " said Lonaker.

"Plutarch." Huck grinned. "I've been a good influence on you." He sniffed the air. "But she can cook, I'll give her that."

"They say the way to a man's heart is through his stomach."

"Well, my stomach thinks my throat's been cut. I could eat a steer with the hide on."

"Go on. I'll watch the payroll."

"You don't have to tell me twice."

Huck fetched his bullwhip from the driver's box. He never went anywhere without it. He entered the station with the twenty feet of braided rawhide riding his shoulder.

Lonaker was climbing into the Concord when two gunshots splintered the sweltering stillness of the afternoon.

He whirled, cross-drawing the Colt Dragoons.

The shots had come from behind the station.

43

Lonaker broke into a run. As Huck and the division agents boiled out of the station's front door, the troubleshooter raced around the corner of the adobe building.

Jute was backing out of the smokehouse. He stumbled, turned, and when he saw Lonaker he opened his mouth to yell. Lonaker saw the gunflash in the dark womb of the smokehouse. Jute flung his arms out, staggered and fell.

Lonaker's first thought was that somehow Sullivan had gotten his hands on a gun.

Then Emily Venard stepped out into the bright heat, and sunlight glanced off the barrel of the pistol in her grasp.

Lonaker felt the cold hatred of her icy gaze. The pistol swung in his direction. He dived to the ground, guns blazing. The bullets slammed the woman backward against the smokehouse wall. She seemed to hang there a moment. The pistol slipped from her fingers and she pitched forward.

The troubleshooter picked himself up, spun on his heel as Huck and the others stampeded around the corner of the station.

"Stay back," he said, and moved with caution to the smokehouse. Kicking her pistol away, he knelt beside Emily Venard, holstering one of the Colt Dragoons. Putting the barrel of the other against the base of her skull, he pressed his fingers into her neck, feeling for a pulse. He knew both bullets had struck her in the chest, but hard-won experience had taught him that sometimes it took more than two bullets to stop a strong person.

Convinced that she was dead, he slipped into the smokehouse, at an angle and in a crouch.

Sullivan was laid out on the stone floor, his shirt front slick with crimson blood. Two shots into the chest at point-blank range—Lonaker could see the black powder burns. The outlaw's face was white as marble, and his breathing was fast and shallow.

As Lonaker bent down, Sullivan's hooded eyes flicked wide open.

"Bitch killed me," he gasped in disbelief.

Lonaker nodded grimly. No question about it. Sullivan was halfway across the river.

"Told you . . . never make it . . . to a judge," whispered Alkali Jim.

Lonaker was angry, mostly at himself. He looked around—at the plate, still covered by the linen, sitting on top of one of the kegs, at the body of Emily Venard beyond the doorway, back at Sullivan. The woman had come in here with cold-blooded murder on her mind. There could only be one reason.

"Who told you about the payroll?" he asked. "It wasn't her. Couldn't have been. Who was it, Sullivan?"

Alkali Jim was fading fast. He couldn't seem to keep his eyes open. He mumbled something. Lonaker couldn't make it out, leaned closer.

"What?"

"Saddlebags . . . picture . . . Molly . . . tell her . . ."

Lonaker heard the death rattle as Sullivan reluctantly let go of his last breath.

The room grew dark. Lonaker looked up to see

Huck filling the doorway, the division agents crowding in behind him.

"What the hell happened?" boomed McGrath.

Tight-lipped, Lonaker didn't answer. He fished the keys to Sullivan's shackles out of his pocket and removed the irons. Standing, he looked down at the dead outlaw for a long moment, seemed to be judging the weight of the shackles in his hand. Sullivan hadn't even had a fighting chance, something Lonaker figured every man deserved, and the troubleshooter felt as though he owed Alkali Jim an apology. He was responsible for the welfare of his prisoner, and he had failed in that responsibility. But it was too late for apologies.

A man who normally kept an iron rein on his emotions, Lonaker lost his temper. He hurled the manacles and leg irons. They struck the stone of the smokehouse wall with a loud clanging. Already on edge, the men at the door jumped.

Huck's eyes narrowed as he watched Lonaker warily. Once again he found himself just a little afraid of this man. Lonaker was a natural-born hunter and slayer of men, and Huck counted society as just plain lucky that the Overland troubleshooter was on its side. If he ever goes bad, decided Huck, I'm getting out of the Territory, and fast.

"What's going on here?" queried McGrath, insistent. He did not know Lonaker as Huck did, and failed to recognize the danger signs. He was bewildered and upset, and he wanted answers.

The sound of a horse at the gallop turned them all around.

"Hey!" yelled Coffman. "It's Fallon!"

Lonaker bulled through them, exploding out onto the sun-blistered hardpack to see Fallon, bent low on a bareback horse, fleeing west along the road.

The troubleshooter raised his pistol, then lowered it without firing a shot. The hostler was already out of short-gun range. Lonaker's thoughts flew to the Sharps-Borschardt in the Concord's guncase. He measured the time it would take to bring the buffalo gun into action against the ground Fallon would cover in that time.

"Grab a horse!" bellowed McGrath. "We'll ride him down!"

"No," said Lonaker. "I'll catch him."

But he didn't move—instead, stood there peering bleakly at the corpse of Emily Venard.

"He's getting away," complained McGrath.

"He won't get far," replied Lonaker.

"I wish somebody would tell me what the hell is going on here," growled McGrath, disgusted.

Lonaker faced him. "This woman killed Sullivan. She got to him on the pretext of bringing him food. Maybe she was going to claim Sullivan attacked her, and she was forced to defend herself. I don't know. She didn't figure on Jute tagging along. But she didn't let that stop her, and she murdered her husband for good measure. She was dead set on getting Sullivan, and nothing was going to keep her from it."

"I knew we had a problem," said Coffman, dumbfounded. "But this . . ." He shook his head. "Do you think she was a member of the Golden Circle?"

"Maybe," said Lonaker. "She was clearly determined to keep Sullivan from talking, and I believe he had some association with the Knights."

"I'm afraid there's more than one bad apple in the Overland barrel," murmured Raney.

"They're well-organized," allowed the trouble-shooter. "Dedicated and dangerous."

"Three people at this station and two of 'em rebel agents," said McGrath, in disbelief. "If it's like this all along the Oxbow, we've lost."

"We may lose," admitted Lonaker, "but not without one hell of a fight."

Chapter Seven

The three horses brought out of Coyote Canyon were still tied to the rear of the Concord. Lonaker went straight to the zebra dun Sullivan had been riding. The division agents came over to stand in a piece of shade provided by the coach. They looked restless and edgy, agitated by the sudden whirlwind of violence they had just witnessed.

Huck entered the station and emerged a moment later with a pick in one hand and a shovel in the other. He made for a spot at the base of the butte, near the sweet-water spring. Shedding his vest, he proceeded to attack the rocky ground with the pick, his powerful muscles rippling in his massive chest and shoulders.

"Hell," grumbled McGrath, after watching the reinsman work for a minute. "Grave-digging isn't one of my favorite pastimes, but I can't just stand here and let him go it alone." He turned to Raney and Coffman. "Why don't you two search the station? Maybe you'll find something."

"What are we looking for?" asked Raney.

McGrath scowled. "We had two rebel spies living

here, Homer. Remember? Copperheads—isn't that what you called them, Phil?"

Coffman nodded. "I doubt either one of them was foolish enough to leave a diary, Sid."

"You never know," said McGrath, and walked off to assist Huck.

Raney and Coffman entered the station.

Lonaker's search of Sullivan's saddlebags unearthed a straight razor, an extra shirt, a block of phosphorous "strike-anywhere" matches, an almost-empty bottle of Taos Lightning, a pistol, a handful of cartridges, and an envelope addressed to James Kincade, General Delivery, Casa Grande.

Opening the envelope, Lonaker found a tintype photograph and a single sheet of stationery.

The beauty of the young woman in the photograph stole Lonaker's breath away. Was this Molly? A shy, sweet smile curved the corners of her mouth. She was in a photographer's studio, sitting in front of a backdrop of what appeared to be the ruins of a Greek temple in a misty woodland.

She wore kid-and-cloth shoes, a balmoral skirt, and a basque waist with delicate lace at the throat. There was something self-conscious about her pose. She sat on the very edge of the chair, hands folded in her lap, feet primly close together. Ringlets of light-brown or auburn hair—it was impossible to say in a tintype—framed a heart-shaped face. Her eyes were bright and inquisitive.

She reminded him of Laura, and the memory was painful. The years did not seem to lessen the pain. It wasn't that she resembled Laura, really. Laura's features had not been so finely sculptured, or her skin so fair. This woman's skin looked smooth and perfect, like porcelain. But Laura had possessed the bloom of inner beauty Lonaker thought he saw in the woman in the photograph.

He put the tintype in the envelope and took out the letter.

Dearest Uncle,
I hope this letter finds you well. I have settled in nicely here. I am pleased with the school. The children are eager to learn. Seven Springs is not so wild and woolly as I imagined it would be.

Though I would dearly love to see you again, it would be unwise of you to come here. The sheriff has your picture on his wall. Your friend Mr. Dockery says he is a Union man, and has it in for all Southerners. I don't think I will ever understand why we can't all live together in peace.

I wish you hadn't asked Mr. Dockery to look out for me. Something about him makes me uncomfortable. He is always coming around. I suppose he takes his obligation seriously. He says there are a lot of rough characters in Seven Springs.

It saddens me when I think of the dangerous life you lead, but I know you are a decent man driven to extremes. Life can be so unfair sometimes. Do take care of yourself and remember always that you are in my heart and thoughts.

With Love,
Molly

Lonaker read the letter twice. Sullivan had been a lucky man, he thought, to have someone like this concerned for him.

Assuming, of course, that the letter could be accepted at face value. The Golden Circle was a secret society operating in a clandestine manner. What if this woman was a member? Sullivan's contact? What if the letter was in fact some kind of secret code, with a hidden message only Sullivan could have deciphered?

Returning the letter to the envelope, Lonaker again looked at the tintype. There was no trace of artifice in her guileless yet beguiling eyes. He couldn't believe this woman had a deceitful bone in her body. Already he had an image of her — an image worth protecting.

Still, the letter produced more questions than answers. She had addressed the letter to James Kincade. If "Kincade" was one of Sullivan's aliases, it was news to Lonaker. And who was this man, Dockery? An outlaw himself? A member of the Knights?

Lonaker decided it was worth a trip to Seven Springs to find out. If nothing else came of it, and assuming Molly really was Sullivan's kin, he could inform her, as gently as possible, of her uncle's death. She had a right to know, and Lonaker felt obliged to tell her, even though he was reluctant to be the bearer of bad tidings.

He double-checked his motives. Was this really a lead worth following? Or was it a desire to see this woman in the flesh?

Maybe it was both. Lonaker smiled thinly. He knew he was going to wind up in Seven Springs, as sure as the sun would rise in the east, and there was nothing to be gained by debating the issue with himself.

But first things first.

He had another lead to follow, and its name was Fallon.

Lonaker climbed into the coach. He shed his broadcloth coat and shrugged into a jacket of tawny buckskin. The jacket was knee-length, with long fringe and beadwork on the shoulders. Next he donned brush-scarred shotgun chaps, and strapped on the crossdraw holsters outside the jacket.

Taking the Henry .44 repeating rifle from the gun case, he loaded it, and grabbed a box of extra rimfire cartridges. From the bench seat he took some dried beef and hardtack, placing this rough and meager fare in a string-tied burlap possibles sack. From the cabinet he procured a half-dozen cheroots and a pair of Vollmer field glasses carried in a hardened case complete with strap. He put the envelope containing letter and photograph in one of his jacket pockets.

Emerging from the coach, he scrutinized the outlaw horses with an experienced eye and settled on the Reno Kid's blazed sorrel. It looked to have a good bloodline and a lot of "bottom." He removed the Kid's long gun, a side-hammer Colt, from the saddle scabbard and replaced it with the Henry. The field glasses and possibles sack were draped over the saddlehorn.

He swung into the saddle and steered the sorrel toward the spring, where Huck and McGrath had finished excavating one shallow grave and were starting on another.

They paused in their labors as he approached. McGrath was glad for a respite. He was a sturdy man, but some years past his prime, and he was already exhausted. He'd removed his coat and left it folded neatly on a rock. His shirt was soaking wet with perspiration, and his face was flushed a deep and unhealthy crimson.

Huck, on the other hand, looked like he was capable of digging deep enough to strike water. Racking the pick on one brawny shoulder, he squinted up at Lonaker. The troubleshooter sat tall and easy in the saddle, against the backdrop of a fireball sun plummeting to the ragged rim of distant purple mountains.

"Going after Fallon," said Huck. It was an observation, not a question.

"Right. When you're finished here, move on. I expect I'll catch him tomorrow, so I should be able to meet you at Painted Rock. But don't wait on me. Get that payroll to Yuma."

Huck nodded. Lonaker reined the sorrel westward, nudging the horse into a swinging canter down the Oxbow road.

"Sounds mighty sure he'll catch up," observed McGrath, "for a man who doesn't look to be in much of a hurry."

"Hurry in this country, you wind up dead," said Huck. "He'll catch Fallon all right. I almost hope he doesn't."

McGrath's glance was sharp with suspicion. "What's that? Fallon's a damned Copperhead spy."

"I know. But I still feel sorry for any man, Copperhead spy or not, who has Lonaker on his trail."

Chapter Eight

Lonaker was an accomplished tracker. He'd learned all the tricks from some of the best in the business. Men like Bridger and Carson had given him lessons. He'd gone from a half-starved orphan stealing just to stay alive on the mean streets of St. Louis and St. Joe to a bona fide plainsman, working first for freighting outfits on the Santa Fe Trail, then as hunter and scout for wagon trains on the Oregon Trail, and finally doing the same for army contingents holding remote frontier outposts.

The first twenty years of his life had been spent on the northern plains. The arid desert of the Southwest was relatively new to him. He'd adapted quickly. James Birch had gone all the way to Fort Laramie to recruit him for the Jackass Line—the prototype for the Overland's Oxbow—in '57. And when Butterfield had won the mail contract a year later, he'd lured Lonaker to the Overland. Now he worked for Wells and Fargo.

The desert was a harsh and unforgiving mistress. Lonaker had learned to survive her cruel and capricious attentions. He did not love it as he had the prairie. Only scorpions and diamondbacks and Apaches loved the desert. But when Birch had made his offer, Lonaker had been past ready for a change of scenery, for Laura had died the previous winter. It seemed as though everywhere Lonaker looked he'd seen something that reminded him of her.

He followed the Oxbow road west. The sun was melting like liquid fire as it plunged to the western rim. The blue shadows of organ pipe cactus and Spanish bayonet slanted long across his path. Right away he detected Fallon's sign. The iron on the left front shoe of the horse Fallon was riding had been deeply scored on sharp rock. Two parallel grooves, like notches on a gun barrel, were plain in the print. This was the signature of Fallon's trail.

The well-traveled road was a dusty river of sign, and sometimes Lonaker lost the trail. When this happened, he dismounted and led the blazed sorrel, his keen gray eyes searching the ground. He did not hurry in his work. A tracker had to be patient, methodical. He did not worry about time, or distance, or the possibility of his prey getting away.

The fourth time he lost the trail, Lonaker couldn't find it in a quarter-mile of road search, so he doubled back, stepping out into the scrub north of the road and heading back to the east, parallel to the road. In this way he cut Fallon's sign where the Copperhead had left the road and struck out across the flats.

From then on Lonaker made better time. Now he did not have to sort Fallon's tracks out of the road clutter. He managed to keep the sorrel at a ground-eating trot more than half the time.

Fallon seemed to be making a beeline for a notch in the range of mountains twenty-odd miles north. These were the Palomas. Lonaker resigned himself to the fact that it would be tomorrow before he himself could reach them.

Sunset filled the hollows of the earth with inky shadows. As the day's heat subsided, the scrub came alive with wildlife. Jackrabbits, roadrunners and coyotes darted through the sagebrush and yucca. He flushed sage hens out of their cover. A red-tailed hawk performed a graceful aerial ballet high overhead, while brush wrens flittered low to the ground. Cholla and ocotillo whipped at his leather-encased legs. Saguaro and the flower stalks of century plants probed the darkening sky, where early stars winked into life.

He came to a shallow draw and found a rock pool, a few inches of brackish water surviving from the last rainfall in the scant shade of gnarled greasewood trees. Snakeweed and mesquite grass grew in the shale of the rocky wash, in pockets of sandy soil. Lonaker circled the site, checking the ground carefully in the last light. Fallon had watered here and pressed on to the northwest, toward the notch in the Palomas.

Lonaker let his horse drink. He himself drank deeply from the Kid's canteen, then filled the canteen from the pool and moved off down the wash a hundred yards to make camp. He knew better than to camp right on top of the water hole. For all he knew it was the only water for fifty square miles, and he did not care to be trod on by hostile Apaches or a manada of wild mustangs while he slept.

Neither did he camp down in the wash. This time of year thunderstorms were common in the mountains, and dry washes many miles out in the flats could be swept by raging flash floods without warning.

He settled for a rock ledge jutting out over the wash. Tying the sorrel's reins to a twenty-pound stone, he let the horse graze the sparse grass. He removed saddle and pad, using the pad to rub the horse down.

Spreading out the Kid's Saltillo blanket, he settled down to dine on jerky and hardtack, washed down with water. He planned to drink his fill tonight and top off the canteen at the rock pool in the morning. Out here a man never knew when the next water source might present itself.

The moon came early, lavishing its ghostly, alabaster light on the desert, softening the land's harsh countenance. Lonaker did not risk a fire, so he used the moonlight to again study the tintype of the woman named Molly.

Even though he knew better.

Sitting there, listening to coyotes serenade the moon, he felt a deep cutting stroke of loneliness. His time with Laura had been too brief. They'd been married less than two years when she died. Those two years seemed like a handful of minutes to Lonaker now. He'd planned on their having a lifetime together. Now he knew that anyone who made such plans was a fool.

For the first twenty years of his life he'd been alone. Twenty years alone against only two years with Laura — he wondered why the last few years since her death had been so difficult. He couldn't seem to adjust to being on his own again. He'd thought it would come easy, having had so much prior experience.

Problem was, a man came to depend on the presence of a woman. A woman's love was habit-forming, and a man got to thinking he couldn't live without it. It smoothed out life's rough edges, and there was no substitute for it. Once a woman filled a man with her love, there was nothing in the world that could cure the emptiness once that love was gone. All a man could do was struggle along, day by day, no longer whole.

The young woman in the tintype struck him as the kind of girl that could make a man proud. Laura had been like that. Married to Laura, Lonaker had felt like the luckiest fellow on God's good earth. Until recently, he hadn't even considered finding another woman to share his life. No one could take Laura's place, but lately he'd been wondering if there wasn't someone out there somewhere who could fill some of that empty space.

There weren't a lot of prospects in these parts. Most of the women who came West did so with their pioneering husbands. Others were broken women with broken dreams and hard eyes who sold their bodies in the towns and mining camps. Not too many nice girls available.

Lonaker put the photograph back in the envelope and called himself a first-class fool. He wasn't so conceited that he thought there might be a chance of striking up a relationship with the schoolteacher of Seven Springs. It wasn't Molly herself, but rather the kind of women he believed she represented, that Lonaker longed for.

Such wishful thinking was folly. He knew that. Worse, it hurt down deep inside. For one thing, he didn't have much of a life to share. He wasn't a good catch. He was a rough and violent man woefully lacking in the social graces. Something about him made decent folk swing a wide loop around him. He saw that, was dismayed by it, and was powerless to do anything about it. People left him alone.

It was the reputation. The killing. Even Huck thought he was a cold-blooded killer. Lonaker supposed it might be true. He hadn't set out to be that way. It just happened. The life he'd chosen put him in harm's way. He'd been in plenty of situations that were kill-or-be-killed, and he didn't hesitate pulling the trigger.

The killing bothered him. He tried not to let it, and he sure never showed it, but every time he took a life he felt as though he surrendered up a piece of his own. Today had been a bad day. He'd killed four people, one of them a woman. He didn't try to ease his conscience by telling himself they'd deserved it. He didn't judge people. Neither did he rationalize it as acts of self-defense. He put himself in those situations of his own free will.

He sometimes thought how nice it would be to live free of such situations. He thought about shucking it all, finding a home somewhere — something new for him. He'd live in peace, with a woman he loved and who loved him. He'd had this notion more and more of late. He looked around these days and saw the country going to hell in a handbasket. There was going to be a lot of killing. Violence was a highly contagious disease and it seemed like everybody had caught a dose of it. A terminal dose. The land was going to run red with blood.

It was about time, mused Lonaker, for sane men to head for tall timber.

He got up and fetched the sorrel. Tying the reins around his left wrist, he rolled up in the Saltillo blanket, with the Henry repeater by his side. He was a long time getting to sleep.

At first light he was on the move again. He lost Fallon's trail only once. He described a wide circle to the west, then swung back around in another circle east, and eventually cut sign. By midmorning he was in the rugged foothills of the Palomas.

The notch proved to be a good pass wedged between steep, pine-clad slopes spotted with sandstone pinnacles, sculptured by a hundred centuries of wind and rain. Sometimes all he had by way of a trail were the fresh scuff marks made by an iron-shod horse on stony ground. But that was enough for Lonaker.

The trail led him up a draw which rose so sharply that he had to dismount and lead the sorrel. It was a strenuous ascent, winding through boulders and fighting to keep his footing in treacherous shale. The draw deposited him onto a high bench scattered with cedar. The faint aroma of woodsmoke cautioned him.

A few minutes later he was deep in a bosky of wind-twisted trees, using the field glasses to get a closer look at a picket shanty poised on the rimrock of a deep barranca. The horse Fallon had taken from the Lime Creek station stood trail-weary in a ramshackle corral of stone and cedar rails. Its head was bowed, and a hind leg was drawn up on the hoof point. Its tail whisked half-heartedly at pesky deerflies.

Lonaker watched the shanty for half an hour. A wisp of smoke trickled out of its rock chimney. Eventually a man emerged to gather an armful of wood from a pile beside the door. It was Fallon. Lonaker made note of the pistol in his belt. Fallon paused to give the tableland a long, careful scrutiny. He failed to see the well-hidden troubleshooter. Lonaker could be as invisible as an Apache when he wanted.

Apparently satisfied that he had this high bench all to himself, Fallon carried the firewood inside.

Lonaker drew the Henry out of its saddle boot and paid a call.

Chapter Nine

This rundown shanty, high and lonesome, might once have been a prospector's shack. There were folks who thought every mountain in this part of the country had to have gold or silver in it. But as Lonaker studied the lay of the land, seeking the best approach, he realized how ideally suited the shanty was for service as an outlaw hideout.

For one thing, it was remote. No one was likely to come up this way if he were just passing through the Palomas range. For another, there wasn't a stick of cover for thirty yards south, east or west. North of the shack was a long drop to the rocky bottom of the barranca. A mountain goat might scale such a precipice. A man couldn't.

The shanty's door faced south. There was a window in the west wall, overlooking the corral. So Lonaker circled wide, the Henry in his grasp, the extra box of rimfires in a pocket of the long buckskin jacket. He moved from tree to tree in a running crouch, coming eventually to the rim of the barranca east of the shack.

Up this high the wind was a constant, the dry hot

breath of the Devil himself, fluting through the canyons and whispering past the peaks and pinnacles. This morning it came from the west, and Lonaker's maneuver put him downwind from the horse in the corral.

He was fifty feet from the shack when Fallon stepped outside again.

Lonaker froze in his tracks. There was no place to hide this close to the rim. All Fallon had to do was look east and the fight was on.

But Fallon was intent on personal business. He unbuttoned his fly and began to make water.

Lonaker thought, I can bring him down with one shot. At this range I can't miss.

But he wanted Fallon alive. He wanted to find out more about the Knights of the Golden Circle, and how many members of that secesh society had already infiltrated the Overland Mail Company. Maybe Fallon didn't know anything. But then again, maybe he knew a lot.

As he relieved himself, Fallon lifted his head and looked casually around.

When he saw Lonaker standing still as a statue fifty feet away, the Copperhead gave a start. Then he yanked the pistol out of his belt and fired, springing toward the shanty door.

The hasty shot whined off the rimrock to Lonaker's right. The troubleshooter moved left, firing the Henry from hip level. The slug bit a chunk out of the picket at the corner of the shack as Fallon dived inside. Gunfire bounced off the flanks of the barranca and rolled away.

Lonaker ran toward the shack, levering another round into the Henry's breech. Fallon stepped back out through the doorway. This time he aimed before firing.

64

Lonaker pulled up and brought rifle stock to shoulder. The two men fired simultaneously.

Fallon's slug struck Lonaker high in the left arm. The troubleshooter distinctly heard the smacking sound the bullet made as it tore into his flesh. The impact turned him, knocking him off balance. It was like being hit with an ax handle, and Lonaker swayed precariously close to the brink of the cliff, his knees suddenly rubbery, his stomach doing a slow roll — natural and involuntary reactions of the body when it knows its been damaged. He felt no pain at first, only a cold, frightening numbness.

Regaining his balance, he worked the lever action of the Henry and looked for Fallon. The Copperhead was sagging against the shanty wall, bent over like a man losing his dinner. Fallon slowly raised the pistol. Lonaker threw himself to the ground, falling on his right side to protect his injured arm. Despite this precaution, bolts of white-hot pain went lancing through him, making him gasp. He heard the deep-throated boom of Fallon's pistol and flinched as the bullet kicked rock dust in his face before ricocheting harmlessly away.

A blister in the rimrock partially sheltered Lonaker, and he squirmed to fit more of his body in the hollow behind this meager protection. He peeked over the blister in time to see Fallon stumble like a drunkard into the shanty. I hit him, thought Lonaker. That makes us even.

Lonaker checked his wound, wincing as his fingers probed the back of his arm and found the bullet's exit hole. The slug had passed through the fleshy portion below the shoulder point. He wiped the blood off his fingers on the sleeve of his buckskin jacket. Nothing serious, he decided. It wasn't his first gunshot wound. Naturally, he hoped it would be his last.

With that in mind, he gave up on the idea of taking Fallon alive. A worthy goal, but it struck him as a lot less worthy than it had ten minutes earlier, and it had never been worth getting killed for. So he proceeded to pepper the shanty with rifle fire. He emptied the Henry's magazine, reloaded, and sent ten more rounds into the shack, some high, some low, some to the left, some to the right. The .44 slugs splintered the shaggy cedar pickets, and Lonaker figured some of them were going through.

Again he reloaded, then counted the rimfires remaining in the box. Nine there, and fifteen in the Henry. He could spend them all, and try to turn the shanty into so much kindling. But Fallon hadn't returned fire. Lonaker wondered if he was still able to.

"Fallon!" he yelled. "Give it up!"

No answer.

Lonaker peered past the shanty, saw the horse in the corral. Would Fallon try to climb out the west window and get to his mount? The troubleshooter breathed a curse. He had to go in. Steeling himself, he got to his feet and walked forward, ready to cut Fallon in half if the Copperhead came out the door with iron in his hand.

But Fallon didn't show. Lonaker paused at the corner of the shanty. The pickets had been carelessly caulked, and the troubleshooter sat on his heels and peered through a crack. It was too bright out here and too dark inside to make anything out. He was keenly aware that Fallon could shoot right through the walls of this ramshackle structure, as he had done. So he moved on to

66

the doorway and barged in, sweeping the Henry laterally from one side of the shack to the other, searching for a target.

Fallon was gone.

Stone floor, a pole roof, a narrow bunk made of leather straps, a rickety table, a couple of empty kegs for sitting on — Lonaker took note of all this in a glance, before his gaze locked onto the small hatch in the back wall, near the floor. The hatch, hinged at the top, was propped open on a stick.

Lonaker stepped to the window in the west wall. The horse stood as before in the corral. No sign of Fallon. The troubleshooter knelt and peered cautiously out through the hatch.

The shanty stood but a few feet from the lip of the precipice. Lonaker crawled out through the hatch, onto this narrow ledge between the shack and a long fall. Then he saw Fallon.

A rope ladder was attached to the back wall of the shanty, its vertical ropes secured around the cedar pickets. It reached a ledge thirty feet below the rim. Fallon was halfway down the ladder. He was having a tough time. Lonaker saw bloodstains on the stout hemp of the ladder.

Lonaker leaned out over the rim and scanned the ledge which traversed the face of the cliff a hundred feet, widening off to the left at the mouth of a cave. Some old sourdough, mused the troubleshooter, had probably found a little color in that cave and figured the mother lode was his for the finding. The set-up he'd left behind was perfect for a man on the dodge. A man like Fallon. Once Fallon got in that cave, Lonaker would need dynamite to get him out.

The Copperhead looked up and saw Lonaker on the rim above. He still had his pistol, and fired a shot at the troubleshooter. Lonaker rocked back as the bullet slapped into the eaves of the shanty. Setting the Henry aside, he drew one of the Colt Dragoons. Putting it right up against one of the ladder's vertical ropes, he pulled the trigger. The slug shredded the hemp. What was left unraveled and came apart with a loud snap. Fallon shrieked in terror, dropping his hogleg and clinging for dear life to the ladder as it swung sideways, spinning him like a top. The pickets to which the remaining vertical rope was attached groaned complaint.

Lonaker peered over the rim. "Fallon!"

Ashen, Fallon looked up. He was still a good fifteen feet above the ledge. The ladder was swinging back and forth like a pendulum, twirling him. Lonaker put the barrel of the Colt Dragoons against the remaining vertical rope.

"No!" screamed Fallon.

The ledge below him was very narrow. If he fell, or jumped, he might make it. But the odds were better that he'd go over the side and plunge to his death. Lonaker wondered just how desperate he was.

"Climb back up," ordered the troubleshooter.

Fallon reached high for a handful of rope, tried to drag himself up.

"I can't!" he yelped. "You gutshot me, you bastard. I'm plumb tuckered out." Again he glanced longingly at the ledge below him.

"Try that and I'll shoot," promised Lonaker.

"Then help me up!" shouted Fallon, angry. "I can't hold on forever, dammit!"

"I want some answers first."

Fallon cursed. "Pull me up or go to hell."

Lonaker considered the task before him. Could he do it, with an injured arm? He flexed the arm experimentally. It was beginning to hurt like hell now, but the bullet hadn't damaged bone or muscle, so the arm hadn't been rendered useless. If he could endure the pain, he might be able to haul Fallon up. All he could do was try.

Holstering the pistol, he braced his back against the wall and tried to find ruts in the rimrock for his bootheels. He spit into the palms of both hands and got a firm grip on the vertical rope.

And pulled.

Hand over hand, inch by laborious inch, he drew Fallon up the face of the cliff, trying to ignore the waves of pain the effort cost him. The Copperhead dangled some fifteen feet below the rim. By the end of it, Lonaker was ready to swear he'd reeled in a good mile of hemp, and that Fallon was carrying anvils in his pockets.

When, finally, Fallon appeared at the rim, Lonaker reached out to grab the man's arm. With one final expenditure of brute strength and sheer tenacity, the Overland troubleshooter dragged Fallon to safety.

The Copperhead lay on his side, knees drawn up tightly, arms clenched around his midsection. His tortured breathing was punctuated with grunts of pain. Sitting against the shanty's back wall, Lonaker wearily drew one of his pistols, put the barrel to Fallon's skull and thumbed the trigger back. The double-click sent a spasm through the Copperhead's body.

"Now you're going to talk," said Lonaker in a fierce whisper. He was at the tail end of his patience. "Or else you're going to learn how to fly."

Chapter Ten

"You're a real sonuvabitch, Lonaker," wheezed Fallon, with feeling.

Lonaker nodded agreement. "I'm glad you know. Because then it'll come as no surprise to you that I'll roll you over the side if you don't talk to me."

"I'm as good as dead anyhow. I got a bullet in my belly." A spasm of pure agony wracked Fallon's body. "Gawd it hurts!" he sobbed. He abruptly swung from self-pity to hateful wrath. "But that suits you, don't it? You like killin', you bloody bastard."

Bloody bastard. Lonaker grimaced, and felt a stab of bitter regret — a little self-pity of his own. Yes, that pretty well described the kind of man he had become, and the truth did not sit well.

"You're wasting time," he said, with no evidence of the compassion he felt for the dying man. "I didn't pull you up just to listen to you bad-mouth me. Are you a member of the Knights of the Golden Circle?"

"Proud of it." Like any man at death's door, Fallon had an inclination to show his true colors.

"Emily Venard — she was too, wasn't she?"

"Yes. Your whole damned precious Overland Mail Company is shot through with Confederates," boasted Fallon.

"What happened to Slim Greaves?"

"Who?"

"The hostler you replaced at the Lime Creek station."

Fallon was either forcing an unpleasant grin or grimacing in pain—Lonaker wasn't sure which.

"She done away with him. Told me she had orders to do it, to make room for me. She's mean as a wolf on a gunpowder diet, that woman."

"Why did she kill Sullivan?"

Fallon writhed, making terrible noises deep in his throat. It took him a moment or two to recover sufficiently to answer.

"Said she'd been told to," he gasped weakly.

"By who?"

"She didn't say. I didn't ask. But I figured it was one of them division agents that was there. I only know a few of the Knights . . ."

Fallon lapsed into a spell of coughing up blood.

The revelation elicited a long, grim silence from Lonaker. McGrath, Raney, Coffman—one of them a Copperhead? Outright denial was the troubleshooter's first reaction. He didn't want to believe it. Fallon was lying. He had to be lying.

Still, it made sense. The Overland division agents were privy to the details of all gold, silver and money shipments through their sections. Who better to inform Sullivan of those details?

If what Fallon said was true, which one was it? Coffman, the Texan? He'd seemed genuinely distressed by the news of secession Lonaker had brought from the Lone Star State. But then, perhaps Phil Coffman was as accomplished an actor as the great tragedians, Edwin Booth and Joseph Jefferson, had proven themselves to be on theater stages back east.

Or maybe Sid McGrath was the inside man. After all, Sullivan had been operating in McGrath's division. But McGrath came across as a man violently opposed to the idea of Southern independence. He'd voted to hang Sullivan from the get-go. Had this merely been a ploy to silence the outlaw with a hemp necktie? Later, McGrath had begged for ten minutes alone with Sullivan, vowing to beat the identity of the informer out of Alkali Jim. He could have harbored ulterior motives. Lonaker wondered if Sullivan would have survived those ten minutes.

Then there was Homer Raney. Lonaker realized he knew little about the man. Raney was a quiet, reserved individual. Until now, all Lonaker had felt he needed to know about Homer was the professionalism Raney demonstrated in handling his job for the Overland. Raney seemed to be committed whole-heartedly to the company. He was all business, and Lonaker could think of no one who knew much of anything about the private side of Homer Raney.

He glanced at Fallon. The Copperhead was white as a boiled shirt. His face was covered with a sheen of cold sweat, and twisted into a snarl of agony.

"Why did you run, Fallon?" asked the trouble-shooter. "You gave yourself away by running."

"I didn't run," whispered Fallon through clenched teeth. He was shuddering uncontrollably now. "Emily Venard sent me to . . ." He cut himself short.

Lonaker pressed harder with the Colt Dragoons, and then it occurred to him that threatening the life of a dying man was ludicrous. He eased off.

"Who did she send you to, and with what message?"

"I'm dying!" whined Fallon pitifully, frightened by the realization that he was done for.

"Where were you going, Fallon?" badgered the troubleshooter. It seemed as though a cold shadow had passed over the Copperhead's features; Lonaker thought he could almost see the life quickly ebbing away. Part of him wanted to let the man go in peace, but the part that wanted all the information he could get out of Fallon while he had the chance won out.

"Seven . . . Seven Springs . . ."

Seven Springs!

If he'd needed justification for his intended visit to that town, Lonaker had it now.

With his last breath, Fallon groaned, "Damn you, Lonaker."

He hacked up more blood, shuddered violently, and was still.

Lonaker eased the hammer down and holstered the Colt Dragoon. Drawing a long, ragged breath, he picked up the Henry repeater, got stiffly to his feet, and walked aimlessly around the shanty. Standing in the doorway, he bleakly surveyed the shack's interior. For a moment his mind was blank, his senses dulled. He felt nothing, saw nothing.

The throbbing pain of his wound brought him back from this limbo. Easing out of the buckskin jacket, he sat on one of the kegs pulled up to the table and ripped the bloody sleeve of his shirt off the injured arm. A label-less brown bottle stood on the table. Lonaker sniffed it. Mescal—distilled pulque, a fermentation from the maguey, or century plant.

The troubleshooter took a long draw of the potent liquor, then poured the rest on his wound, hissing through clenched teeth as the mescal burned like liquid fire. He watched blood-tinged drops of mescal leave his fingers to puddle on the stone floor.

He used the torn sleeve as a makeshift bandage, pulling it tight as he could stand. Feeling drained and a little dizzy, he sat there for a spell and let his gaze roam idly over the shanty. This was a lonely place, he thought. The hot dry wind whistled through chinks in the picket walls, moaned beneath the eaves. He wondered how Fallon had come to know of this place. He wondered about Fallon himself. If the Copperhead had been an outlaw before playing the role of Overland hostler, he'd somehow managed to keep himself out of Lonaker's bible. And why, when he'd been on an errand—presumably an important errand—to Seven Springs, located in the Big Maria Mountains a long day's ride to the northwest, had he bothered to tarry here?

Nothing in the shanty provided a clue, so Lonaker stirred up some energy and walked out to the corral. The horse whickered softly and watched him with lachrymal brown eyes. In his haste to flee the Lime Creek station, Fallon had not bothered with a saddle. The horse still wore its bridle. Rein leather dragged the ground.

Lonaker propped the Henry against a pole and draped his good arm over the top post of the cedar corral. As he took a long look around, the horse strolled over and nudged him with its velvet-soft muzzle.

"Don't worry," murmured Lonaker. "I won't leave

you here in this godforsaken place."

He checked the sun, a blaze of white heat in the pallid blue dome of the sky, and calculated the time of day as accurately as any keywinder could. If he intended to catch Huck at the Painted Rock station, he was going to have to cover a lot of ground in a big hurry.

He tried to shake off an uncharacteristic lethargy. What was the matter with him? A little soul-searching provided the answer. Defeatism. Something new for him. Events of the last two days had unveiled a secessionist conspiracy to undermine the Overland Mail Company, and Lonaker was doubting his ability to thwart it.

Lonaker was a fighter. He'd fought for survival in the streets and alleys of St. Louis as a homeless child. He'd fought hostile Plains Indians, and the prairie itself, as a hunter and scout. He'd spent the last few years fighting the road agents who pestered the Oxbow Route. But how could he fight something as insidious as the Knights of the Golden Circle? You had to see your enemy to fight him.

Shaking his head, Lonaker reproached himself. Even if the cause was hopeless, the fight was still worth fighting. He'd been hired to do a job, and whether or not the job was impossible didn't enter into it. He'd killed a man today, and been wounded in the process—he put these down as the reasons for his self-doubt.

A length of coiled rope was hanging on one of the upright posts. Lonaker walked over to fetch the hardtwist, intending to use it to lead Fallon's horse back to the Oxbow. The animal was Overland property, after all. As he reached for the rope he saw the heavy iron single-block, attached by its massive hook to the upright

75

where the bottom pole crossed. The rim of the barranca was only a couple of long strides away. He took those strides and peered over the edge. As he had guessed, the entrance to the cave was almost directly below the corral.

Was there something cached down there? There must have been at one time. This block-and-tackle rig had been employed to haul something up or lower something down. He could use the rig to lower himself to the ledge. But was it worth the effort, and the risk?

Lonaker measured his curiosity against the strength he had left, and decided to take a look.

Chapter Eleven

Running the rope through the block, he looped one end and made a stirrup hitch. He sat on the rim, carried the rope over his left shoulder, across his back and under the right arm. Dropping the end that wasn't looped over the side, he confirmed that it was long enough to reach the ledge. His attention strayed from the ledge to the bottom of the barranca. He felt second thoughts coming on and headed them off. Securing one foot in the stirrup, he slid off the rim, holding on to the rope for all he was worth.

The hard-twist burned through his hands. He was dropping too fast! He tightened his grip, ignoring the pain caused by the rope flaying his palms, and slowed his descent.

Dangling a few feet below the rim, he tried to haul himself back up, and when he found he could do so, felt a lot better about the situation and began letting himself down the side of the cliff.

The single-block's pulley screeched. Plucked like a fiddle string on the rock, the taut rope hummed. Lonaker found himself beginning to spin, and used his free leg to brace against the cliff face.

At first he watched the ledge which — he hoped — was his destination. Before long he'd decided it wasn't a good idea to look down. No matter how hard he tried to focus on the ledge, his eyes seemed to have a will of their own, and kept straying to the bottom of the canyon. He discovered he was better off concentrating on the face of the cliff at eye level.

Reaching the ledge, he breathed a heartfelt sigh of relief, winced as he flexed aching fingers. The shelf was treacherously narrow, so he wasted no time in slipping foot out of stirrup and sidling into the cave.

The entrance was roughly four feet in diameter, and he could see it had been widened, long ago, with pick and chisel. Once inside, he found the ceiling inclined sharply, so that he could stand almost erect.

The interior was cool and dark; but not so dark he couldn't see — and what he saw was the stuff wars were made of. Kegs of Dupont gunpowder were stacked to his right. To his left were cases of ready-made cartridges and crates which looked like small coffins.

The cave was twenty feet deep, and in the back were stashed saddles and bridles, stacks of brown wool blankets, tins of hardtack and coffee, several Sibley tents neatly folded.

He used a tent spike to pry the lid off one of the crates. Though he was almost certain he knew what the crates contained, he just had to see for himself.

Rifles. British Enfields, .577 caliber, with the brass mountings which distinguished them from American-made Springfields. Twenty rifles to the crate, an even dozen crates. He checked one of the cartridge boxes.

The cartridges were also of British manufacture, seventy grains of powder, a 530-grain lead bullet.

Lonaker stood for several minutes in the center of the cave, his brooding gaze taking in every detail of this hidden arsenal.

Full-fledged war had come to the Territory.

Obviously the secessionists were plotting to take this part of the country by force.

He wasn't dealing with a gang of outlaws and malcontents — he saw that now. No, this was a carefully orchestrated insurgency.

He realized the conspiracy to deal the Overland a death blow was sound military logic. The rebels intended to cut their enemy's line of communication and supply — the Oxbow Route. In this way they would effectively isolate the federal garrisons at Fort Yuma and a handful of other posts in the region. Their people had already infiltrated the Overland and had already begun to wreak havoc from within. And when the time was right this secret cache — and how many more like it? — would be drawn from to arm the insurrectionists.

The discovery of these supplies stashed high in the remote Palomas fired a slow-burning anger in the troubleshooter. These Knights of the Golden Circle were no better than backshooting cowards in his book. They lacked the guts to declare themselves and fight their foes like men, face-to-face.

Somehow he was going to stop them.

But how?

Destroying this cache would be a good place to start.

With Lonaker, thought quickly turned into action. He smashed in the top of a powderkeg with his bootheel and tipped the keg over, spilling what he'd heard

Plains Indians call "black sand." He broke open a second keg, and with its contents laid a trail of powder across the stone floor of the cave and out onto the shelf.

He hauled himself back up to the rimrock. Fetching an armful of kindling from the shanty's woodpile, he built a fire near the edge of the cliff. While it caught, he led Fallon's horse to the bosky where the blazed sorrel was tethered. He deposited the Henry repeater in its saddle boot, then returned to the shanty to retrieve his buckskin jacket. The fire was blazing now. He selected a burning brand and dropped it over the side, aiming for the trail of black powder on the ledge. The brand struck the shelf and caromed off, showering sparks. The sparks ignited the powder. When he saw the puff of white smoke, Lonaker turned and ran for all he was worth.

He'd made a dozen running strides when, with a deafening explosion, the ground beneath his feet quaked violently, pitching him to hands and knees. Several more loud blasts shook the earth, followed by a staccato crackling as hundreds of cartridges were detonated. Lonaker looked over his shoulder at a geyser of white smoke, streaked with plumes of black, billowing out of the barranca on a surging updraft, to be shredded and curled by a crosswind sweeping over the rimrock.

The troubleshooter picked himself up and brushed himself off.

"War's been declared," he murmured, and bent his steps for the bosky where the horses were waiting.

It took him the rest of the day to reach his rendezvous

with Huck at Painted Rock, fifty miles west of the Lime Creek Station on the Oxbow. As the sorrel splashed across the rocky shallows of the Gila River, Lonaker peered through the purple shadows of dusk and saw his custom-made Concord in front of the station house. The hostler, a towheaded youngster who looked like he'd just come off the farm, was helping Huck unhitch the lathered team. They left off and walked out to meet the troubleshooter.

"See you caught him," remarked Huck, eyeing the horse Lonaker was leading by the leathers. "Left him for the buzzards, as usual, I suppose."

"Some things never change."

"Looks like he winged you."

"It's nothing."

Lonaker watched two men emerge from the lamp-lighted interior of the adobe station. One was the Painted Rock agent, a paunchy ex-vaquero named Sancho. The other was Coffman.

"Phil's riding with you?" Lonaker asked Huck.

The reinsman nodded. "Since I'm carrying the payroll he thought he'd keep me company, instead of taking the regular westbound."

As Lonaker dismounted, Sancho waddled over, wearing the ear-to-ear grin that was his trademark. Seldom was he seen without that foolish grin. But Lonaker knew he was no fool. And he wasn't as soft as he might appear at first glance. Sancho was a true *hombre del campo*.

"*Señor* Lonaker! It is good to see you again. *Como está usted?*"

"*Muy bien, amigo. Como está su esposa?*"

"*Ojalá!*" exclaimed the station agent, shaking both

hands, as though he'd scorched his fingers on a hot stove. He launched into a rapid-fire tirade regarding the faithless harlot whom he was cursed to love.

Lonaker smiled tolerantly, and pretended to pay attention, though he'd heard it all before. Sancho's unusual marital situation was the talk of the Oxbow. His wife lived across the border. Sancho claimed they dared not live together. *Madre de Dios,* they would end up killing each other if they tried! He had nothing nice to say about her, and apparently she wasn't one to sing his praises, either.

Nonetheless, Sancho was known to slip across the border now and again, whenever his duties permitted. No one needed to be told what took place on those occasions. Sancho's thirteen children, who lived with their mother, were living testimonials.

It was a tradition among Overland drivers to provoke Sancho into his vociferous harangue about his wife, and Lonaker played the game too, knowing Sancho would be hurt if he did not.

Lonaker listened politely for a moment, then turned to Coffman as the division agent drew near. Sancho took charge of Lonaker's mount and Fallon's horse. He walked them to the corral, still playing chin music. Once incited he needed no audience, and Lonaker figured he'd carry on for at least a half-hour.

"Where's Fallon?" asked Coffman, staring at the bloodstained sleeve of the troubleshooter's buckskin jacket. "Did you kill him?"

"Yes."

"He was a Copperhead, wasn't he?" Coffman shook his head. "My God, the Overland is reeking with secessionists, John. Did you find out anything?"

Lonaker made a snap judgment not to confide in Coffman. He couldn't trust anyone, except Huck.

"I found out he was hard to kill. That's about all."

"Well, we didn't find any clues back at Lime Creek. I didn't think we would. I'm heading back to my division. Hitched a ride with Huck. They might still want to get their hands on the payroll."

"I reckon that's so."

Coffman went back into the station. The hostler was leading the team to the corral. Huck was dutifully applying grease from a dope pot to Betsy's axles. Lonaker climbed into the coach, stiff and sore. He slacked wearily onto the upholstered seat. Firing up a cheroot, he savored the tobacco's pungent bite. His slate-gray eyes, narrowed against the blue smoke, were fixed on the strongbox at his feet.

Later, Huck poked his head into the coach. "Are you all right?"

Lonaker nodded, deep in thought.

"Sancho's fixed up some beans and tortillas. Are you hungry? I sure am. I'm hungrier than a coyote with a toothache."

"Go on. I'll be in."

Huck nodded and turned for the station, carrying his ever-present bullwhip.

Lonaker finished the cheroot and flicked the butt out a window. With a long sigh, he pulled out the cabinet's sliding leaf. He took a sheet of vellum from one of the drawers, a steel-point pen and a bottle of India ink from another, and proceeded to write a letter explaining why he was about to steal the Fort Yuma payroll.

Chapter Twelve

Prior to finishing his letter to Huck, Lonaker gave a map of the area around Seven Springs long and careful study. It was hard to make a definite plan of action. He had no way of knowing what might happen in the coming days as a direct result of the action he was taking. The best he could do was work it out based on what he hoped to accomplish. With this in mind, and calculating time and distance in relation to the map, he wrote the letter's final two lines. He signed it *Your friend, John*.

He folded the sheet of vellum, slipped it into an envelope, wrote Huck's name on the front. Your friend. He smiled pensively. His friendship would probably become the source of a great deal of embarrassment for Huck, not to mention persecution. He wasn't concerned for himself, or for his own reputation. Desperate times required desperate measures. But he did worry about Huck, and what might happen to him.

In the end, he decided personal considerations could not be permitted to sway him. He had a job to do. So did Huck. The ex-prizefighter had signed on knowing full well there were risks involved. He'd put his life on the line for the Overland Mail Company on numerous occasions. This time Lonaker was asking just a little more. This time Huck would be putting his good name on the line.

And for men like Huck Odom, honor was more important than life itself.

"Sorry, old friend," murmured Lonaker. "I wish I could think of another way."

He slipped the envelope into a pocket of his buckskin jacket, put away the pen and ink and the sliding leaf. From a bottom drawer he took a brass ring laden with skeleton keys. He tried the keys one at a time in the strongbox padlock. With the sixteen keys on the ring, he could open almost any lock he happened across. The fourth key worked.

The payroll was carried in four canvas sacks stamped U.S. Army. Lonaker took empty saddlebags from the seat compartment and placed two money sacks in each pannier. He closed and locked the strongbox.

His conscience nagged without mercy. When he risked his life it was his business, but did he have the right to risk the Army's money? But if he didn't prevent the secessionists from shutting down the Overland, more than Army money would be in jeopardy. The forts, and the soldiers manning those posts, would be at the mercy of the rebels.

Lonaker put the saddlebags back under the seat and climbed out of the coach. Taking a deep breath and squaring his shoulders, he walked into the station.

Sancho, Huck, Coffman and the young hostler were eating at a long trestle table in the common room. Lonaker sat down, had a cup of coffee, a couple of tortillas, and a modest serving of Sancho's renowned *frijoles*.

Sancho spiked his beans with chiltipiquin peppers and wild onions. They were, as Huck had once blissfully declared, hot enough to melt the wax in a man's ears. Many were the Overland drivers who relished a meal stop at Painted Rock just for a bellyful of Sancho's beans.

As usual, Huck was shoveling grub with enthusiasm. He paused only long enough to ask the troubleshooter if they were moving on tonight.

"We'll leave in the morning," replied Lonaker. "Should make Yuma by midafternoon."

He didn't eat much. It wasn't that he didn't like the fare. He had an iron constitution. But tonight he lacked an appetite.

"I'll take the first watch," volunteered Huck, as he transferred another heaping helping of beans from the big iron pot in the middle of the table to his plate. "You look like you've burned up all your coal. Better get some sleep."

Lonaker nodded. Sancho had brought the Henry repeater in, so he picked up the rifle and went into the next room. A half-dozen narrow bunks lined one wall, three up and three down. A kerosene lamp on a wooden trunk beneath the only window illuminated the room. The window was open, and the cooling breath of the night sluggishly stirred the grain-sack curtains. Lonaker turned the lamp down and stretched out fully clothed on one of the lower bunks.

Coffman and the hostler came in a little later. The kid stripped down to his long johns and climbed into the bunk above Lonaker. The troubleshooter pretended to be asleep. Coffman shed coat and boots and groaned wearily as he lay down on one of the other lower bunks. In a matter of minutes he was sawing logs. Lonaker listened to the kid's breathing and knew exactly when the young man fell asleep.

But he couldn't sleep himself. Too many thoughts in his head. He stared at the bottom slats of the overhead bunk and waged war with second thoughts.

Would it work? He asked himself that question a hundred times. Life held no guarantees. But he couldn't fight an enemy if he didn't know who the enemy was. The secessionists were pretending to be honest, law-abiding, Union-loving citizens. What was that old saying? You had to fight fire with fire.

Lonaker could play their game. The Golden Circle was infiltrating the Overland. Fine. He would infiltrate the Golden Circle. The payroll would buy him into the society. Guns and ammunition, like those he had destroyed up in the Palomas Mountains, cost money. He was counting on the Knights having a real need for the payroll.

It was the only trail he could take that would lead him to the identity of the man he was after.

Coffman, Raney or McGrath.

After cleaning up the supper mess, Sancho entered the sleeping room, blew out the lantern, and took the last available lower bunk. Lonaker listened to him mumble his prayers. Sancho was a good man. A God-fearing man. Could he be trusted? Lonaker knew he had no choice. His plan required him to rely on the station agent. It was one of those variables that rendered his plan so fraught with risk.

In such matters a man had to measure the odds and then make his bets. Like poker. You never knew for sure what cards your opponent held close to his vest. Lonaker was gambling that the Mexican wouldn't have a stake in the cause of Southern independence. Unlike so many other Overland employees, he did not hail from Texas or one of the slave states farther east. Pretty thin ice to walk on, but Lonaker was short on options.

The night dragged on endlessly. Lonaker endured two hours on the bunk, and when he couldn't stand another minute, cat footed into the common room.

Sancho kept a pot of coffee on the stove at all times. The fire in the woodburner's black iron belly had died down to a bed of orange embers, but the coffee was still plenty warm. Lonaker poured himself a cup, lit a cheroot, and took a seat at the long trestle table, staring into the darkness.

An hour later he stepped outside, rifle in hand, to find Huck sitting with his back against the adobe wall of the station. The moon was about to set. A glance at the stars told Lonaker it was close to midnight. He turned to the brawny reinsman and nodded at the station house door.

"Get some shut-eye. I'll take over."

Huck got to his feet, stretched, and growled at cramped, complaining muscles. He looked like a grizzly bear getting up on its hind legs, ready to attack. Lonaker felt another stab of keen regret as he watched the ex-prizefighter. Huck had been a good friend. The trouble-shooter was sorry for the tribulation he knew was going to descend on this man.

"How's the arm?" asked Huck.

"Hurts like hell."

The reinsman stepped to the door, paused on the threshold, brow furrowed.

"The Overland's in big trouble, isn't it?"

Lonaker nodded, his eyes probing the desert night.

Huck slapped the bullwhip against his thigh. "Well, I

don't think they've invented the trouble we can't handle, Mr. Lonaker."

"Just watch your back," advised Lonaker. "Remember, you can't trust anybody. He might be a Copperhead."

"You're not. I trust you. See you in the morning. I'm going to get some of that sleep 'that knits up the raveled sleeve of care.' Shakespeare."

Lonaker turned slowly and watched Huck disappear into the black womb of the station.

He waited a half-hour before moving, silent as shadow, to the open window of the sleeping room. Huck's distinctive, wall-shaking snore was drowning out Coffman. Lonaker crossed the hardpack to the Concord, retrieved the saddlebags filled with the Army payroll, and headed for the corral.

The Reno Kid's saddle and bridle were in a shed which served as tack room. Lonaker draped the saddle and the saddlebags on the corral's top pole and climbed over to move slowly through the fourteen horses in the pen. He murmured sweet nothings to keep them calm. He caught up the blazed sorrel without undue trouble, and slipped the bridle over its head. The horse balked some accepting the bit. Lonaker twisted its ear and kept matters under control.

Leading the horse over to the saddle, he noticed Sancho standing on the other side of the corral fence. The station agent was watching him impassively.

"Been expecting you," said the troubleshooter. "You sleep light."

"*Si, Señor* Lonaker." Sancho shrugged. "Pistoleros and Apache broncos have been trying to sneak up on me all my life."

Lonaker draped the saddle over the horse and cinched up.

"What's the best way to fight an Apache, Sancho?"

Sancho was an authority on the subject. "Only one way, if you want to live. You must think like an Apache. Move like an Apache. Fight like an Apache. If you don't, you will surely die."

Lonaker nodded. "I'm not fighting Apaches this time. But the men I'm up against are just as cunning. I figure my only chance against them is to be more cunning than they are." He tied off the latigo over the front rigging ring, dropped the fender and turned to the station agent. "I have a big favor to ask of you."

"Anything."

Lonaker gave him the letter addressed to Huck. "I want you to make sure Huck gets this. But don't give it to him in the morning. I reckon he'll go on to Yuma, with Coffman. Wait until the next day, then ride after him."

Sancho took the letter. "I will do as you ask."

"The kid can watch this place while you're gone. Whatever you do, don't let anyone but Huck get that letter." As he fitted boot to stirrup he had a thought. "Wait. If you can't find Huck in town, try the army post. If he's there, or if you can't find him, you can give up the letter to Colonel Dahlgren."

Sancho nodded. Lonaker swung into the saddle. The station agent lowered the gate pole.

"*Buena suerte,* Señor Lonaker."

"Thanks," said Lonaker as he rode by. "I'll need all the luck I can get."

Sancho watched him go until the night swallowed him up.

Chapter Thirteen

The town of Yuma had grown to maturity under the protective wing of the federal fort, where the mighty Colorado plunged out of the mountains and twisted like a gigantic brown serpent through the malpais on its way to the border.

The fort, an orderly arrangement of stone and adobe buildings, stood on high ground overlooking the settlement. Standing grim and alone a mile out on the flat was the hulking eyesore of the territorial prison.

With the Army post, the prison and the Oxbow Route, Yuma flourished. It was a rough and ready town, providing recreation for soldiers, prison guards and the lusty men who worked the mining and lumber camps in the mountains to the north.

As he rode into town at the head of a five-man detail—one sergeant and four troopers—Colonel Eric Dahlgren cast a jaundiced eyed upon the place. Afternoon heat shimmered off the hardpack of the wide street, deeply scored by wagon and *carreta* wheels.

A man could break both legs trying to walk across a Yuma street, reflected Dahlgren. And on the infrequent occasions when it rained, these same streets became treacherous quagmires of rust-colored mud. A whiskey peddler, drunk on his own snakehead, had drowned in that alley over there, one stormy night last year.

A perfect example of poetic justice, mused the colonel, a career soldier who held civilians generally in low esteem. He was willing to concede that there were a few worth their salt. But he didn't think any of them resided in Yuma.

Dahlgren fished a handkerchief out of a pocket of the white linen duster he wore to protect his uniform, and mopped the sweat off his face. His features were hawkish. His eyes, the cloudy green color of the fjords in his native Scandinavia, could cut through a man like a saber stroke.

The colonel was a highly intelligent, impeccably honest, and well-educated man. As a naive youth he had believed the poets and philosophers when they waxed eloquent about mankind's limitless potential for greatness. A lifetime of experience since then had plucked the scales from his eyes. He couldn't abide rapacity or stupidity in others. And Yuma was full to the brim with ignorant, greedy people.

He saw them now, in the open windows and doorways and in the scant shade on both sides of the street. Cardsharps, prostitutes, drummers, merchants. All of them preyed on his soldiers. Worse, they held the Army in ill-disguised contempt. It was better to receive a compliment rather than a curse from the thief who picked your pocket.

But these civilians scorned and slighted Dahlgren's soldiers. Until there was danger—until the Apaches embarked on a bloody raid, or bandit gangs started raising hell along the border, or prisoners broke out of the prison. Then the civilians howled for protection from the garrison.

I may not have much of a garrison left, thought Dahlgren, when my men learn that six months of pay in arrears has been stolen.

But the Army got what it deserved, in his opinion, when it placed its affairs in the hands of civilians.

The colonel reined his horse around a corner at the intersection of the garrison road with Yuma's main street. The detail trailed along behind. Now Dahlgren could see the crowd congregated in front of the adobe structure housing the Overland's office — between twenty and thirty men, peeking through the front windows, filling the boardwalk, spilling out into the street.

They all seemed to be talking at once, an irritating babble, but every man fell silent as Dahlgren steered his mount to a tie-rail in front of the Overland office. They knew better than to fire a lot of tiresome questions at the Fort Yuma commanding officer. Dahlgren was better known for his temper than his tolerance.

Like the Red Sea parting, they made a path for him as he crossed the boardwalk. At the door, he turned to peruse the crowd with stern disfavor, then glanced at the sergeant who, with the four troopers, was still mounted.

"Macready."

"Yes, sir."

"Move them."

"Yes, sir!"

The three-striper dismounted with alacrity and bulled his way through the throng with exuberance. The civilians tried to get out of his way, but the burly

Irish noncom would not be denied his fun. He knocked one man aside with an elbow. "Excuse me, sir," he said, smiling like a leprechaun. He sent a second man staggering with another cheery apology.

Gaining the boardwalk, Macready turned to block the door through which the colonel had just passed. The sergeant planted big fists on his hips and slowly scanned the crowd.

"Now gentlemen," he said, rolling the words with a thick brogue. "I know ye must have better things to do than to be lollygaggin' out here in the hot sun. So I must ask ye to be on your way."

No one moved. Macready breathed a melodramatic sigh, whipped the pistol out of the flap holster at his side, and fired a round into the sky.

The civilians scattered like quail.

Macready watched their flight with profound gratification.

"Flamin' rabble," he murmured.

Dahlgren was met in the front room by a lanky, sandy-haired man wearing a tin star on his vest.

"Afternoon, Colonel. I sent word up to the fort soon as . . ."

"Where are they, Sheriff?"

"Back room."

Dahlgren passed through the swinging gate of a counter, through another door. Long benches lined the walls to left and right. Across the room was a door leading outside. The doorway was filled by the bulk of the town's deputy sheriff. He was tilted against the frame, a shotgun cradled in his arms.

Through a window in the rear wall Dahlgren could see the Overland "yard," encircled by a high adobe wall.

Half of the yard was a corral, where two dozen horses were bunched around a water trough in the shade of an old oak. The only decent shade, mused the colonel, for twenty square miles. In the other half of the yard stood a mud wagon and, closer to the back door, a dust-covered Concord coach.

As Dahlgren entered, one of two men sitting on the bench to the colonel's left jumped up.

"Colonel, I'm Phil Coffman. I . . ."

"I know." Dahlgren spared him the merest glance and turned to the other man. "You're Lonaker's driver, aren't you?"

Huck Odom sat leaning forward with his head down and hands clasped between his knees. He didn't look up.

"That's right. Huck Odom."

"Where is he?"

"I don't know."

"I can't believe it," declared Coffman. "I never thought John Lonaker would turn bad. Colonel, I promise you the Overland will do everything in its power to . . ."

Dahlgren impatiently raised a hand to cut Coffman short. "Mr. Odom, am I to believe you were unaware of Lonaker's intentions?"

Tight-lipped, Huck slowly raised his head. He met Dahlgren's steely gaze without flinching.

"I'm still unaware of his intentions," said the reinsman, his tone as flat as the bottom of a frying pan.

"They should be obvious to you. They certainly are to me."

Hands clasped behind his back, the colonel began to pace restlessly, spurs ringing against the floor. He paused once to peer curiously at the bullwhip looped over the deputy sheriff's shoulder.

"That yours?" asked Dahlgren.

"No," said Huck. "It's mine, and I'd like it back."

"Why are we being detained, Colonel?" queried Coffman.

"I want to know what happened. I want some answers."

"I wish I had some for you. Lonaker showed up at the Lime Creek station day before yesterday. He had the payroll with him. Said the westbound had broken down, and he'd taken charge of the strongbox. A gang of outlaws waylaid him in Coyote Canyon. They were after the payroll, and were expecting the westbound. Lonaker killed three of them and took Alkali Jim Sullivan prisoner. He brought Sullivan to Lime Creek in irons.

"The wife of the Lime Creek station agent, Emily Venard, murdered Sullivan. Shot her husband, too. Lonaker killed her. The hostler, a man known as Fallon, made a run for it. He and Emily Venard were Copperheads. It seems the Overland has more than its fair share of secessionists on the payroll. We're going to have to weed them out."

"Why did this woman kill Sullivan?"

"Someone was informing Sullivan about our gold and money shipments. Someone inside the company. She killed Sullivan to silence him. To protect the identity of the inside man." Coffman glanced angrily at Huck. "Now I guess we know who that inside man was."

"What happened then?" asked Dahlgren.

"Lonaker went after Fallon. Told Huck to go on to

96

Painted Rock. I rode along to help guard the payroll. Lonaker showed up last night, said he'd tracked down and done for Fallon. This morning we woke up to find him and the payroll gone. I tried to track him. But I lost his trail right off, in the Gila. He rode into the river and I never could find where he came out."

Dahlgren had stopped pacing now, and stood gazing out the window. For a moment, no one spoke. All eyes were on the colonel.

At length, he said, "I guess we all got caught with our pants down. I thought John Lonaker was a man of integrity. The kind of man that's all too rare out here. I suppose this proves every man has his price." He turned to the sheriff, who stood in the doorway to the front office. "You have some work to do at the telegraph office, don't you, Sheriff?"

"I'll wire the sheriff of every town that's got a telegraph." He glanced at Coffman and Huck. "What about these two?"

"Mr. Coffman is free to go."

"Good," said the division agent. "On my own authority, I'm going to offer a reward for Lonaker, dead or alive. I'll have some posters printed up."

"Fine," said the colonel. "Mr. Odom, you'll be my guest at the fort for the time being."

Huck got wearily to his feet. Dahlgren thought he looked like a man who'd lost his best friend. Maybe that was the case. Maybe Huck hadn't played a willing part in Lonaker's larceny. But he'd been the trouble-shooter's man for years now. Guilt by association.

"Guest," said Huck dryly. "You mean prisoner."

"Consider it to be for your own protection. Once Coffman's 'paper' gets out, you'll have bounty hunters

97

dogging your heels, hoping you'll lead them to Lona-ker. And you've got my soldiers to worry about. They haven't been paid in six months, and thanks to your friend, it doesn't look like they will be for another six. A soldier doesn't ask for much, but when he doesn't get his thirteen dollars a month, he's trouble on two legs."

Huck didn't look too impressed. "I guess I ought to thank you, Colonel, for being so concerned."

Dahlgren's smile was cold enough to freeze a bullet.

"You strike me as an educated man, Mr. Odom. So you should know that bad things happen to those who keep bad company."

Chapter Fourteen

Lonaker reached Seven Springs a day and a half after leaving the Painted Rock station.

Had he been in the mood for scenery, he might have appreciated the approach into town, down a sagebrush valley hemmed in by the foothills at the southern end of the Big Maria Mountains. To either side rose steep slopes thick with conifers, beneath higher reaches of fractured rock. The valley narrowed like the neck of a bottle as it neared the Colorado River. Seven Springs was the cork.

But Lonaker wasn't much in the mood. Ordinarily, he didn't worry about something once it was done. This time, though, he had a feeling he'd stuck his neck out too far. He'd gotten into the habit of throwing looks over his shoulder, checking his back trail. This being on the dodge didn't sit well.

Seven Springs was a small community—a couple of streets lined with adobe and raw clapboard buildings. Its existence hinged on the mining and lumber concerns which were just beginning to take hold in the mountains. Not only the Big Marias, but also the Palo Verde and Mule ranges to the south, as well as the Sawtooths and Buckskins farther north. Beyond the mountains to the west, across the Colorado, was the uncharted wasteland called the Mojave Desert.

The town was also a supply point for the stern-wheelers which plied the Colorado between Yuma and Callville, Nevada. Most goods were brought to Seven Springs on the river.

A mile east of town, Lonaker struck a road that curled on up into the foothills, and met an oldtimer driving a spring wagon. The wagon was loaded with supplies, and Lonaker assumed they were earmarked for some remote camp in the high country. The driver hauled back on the leathers to stop the mule team.

"Howdy, stranger."

Lonaker touched the brim of his hat, and while he was at it, pulled it down a little lower over his face.

"Wonder could you help me?" he asked. "I'm looking for the schoolhouse."

"That ain't no hill for a stepper," drawled the other. He tucked his quid of shag tobacco into a cheek and spat a stream of brown juice between the flanks of the last two hardtails in the hitch. "It's the first place you'll come to, iffen you stick to this hyar road. Now, iffen you fall into the Colorado, you know you done gone too fur."

Lonaker heard a wheezing noise, reminiscent of a squeaky blacksmith's bellows. The driver's bony shoulders were shaking, and the troubleshooter realized the man was laughing at his own witticism.

"I'm obliged," he said. "And I'll try not to get my feet wet."

"How come you want to know, stranger? You 'pear to be a mite long of tooth for schoolin'."

Lonaker smiled tolerantly. "Just passing through. Got a message to deliver."

This enigmatic response only piqued the old-timer's curiosity. He cocked his head to one side and flashed a sly yellow grin.

"Could it be the schoolteacher and not the schoolin' yore after?"

"Thanks again," said Lonaker, and rode on.

The driver turned to watch him go. "Cain't blame you, son," he called after the troubleshooter. "Why, iffen I war thirty year younger I'd set my cap fur the little lady myself. Gee-up! You lazy, no-account, lop-eared, wall-eyed, swaybacked knockheads, hyaw!"

The blistered whitewash was peeling like dead skin off the schoolhouse's sun-warped clapboard. Windows on two sides, and a door on a third, were open. As he drew near, Lonaker heard a woman's voice, soft and lyrical. Through one of the windows he saw children seated on benches at long split-log tables. A few glanced his way. He dismounted at the front corner of the building, sat on his heels with the reins in his hands, eyes narrowed as he listened, fascinated, to her voice.

But he grew old
This knight so bold
And o'er his heart a shadow
Fell as he found
No spot of ground
That looked like Eldorado . . .

Lonaker rubbed his whisker-bristled jaw and wondered if it wouldn't be better to make himself more presentable before meeting Molly. Then he laughed softly at himself. Why was he so worried about making a good impression? He was the bearer of bad news. And an outlaw, besides. He was hardly some young beau come a-courtin', and he told himself to keep a firm grip on the cold handle of that reality.

But the voice stirred the ashes of longing deep inside him. Again, painfully, he was reminded of Laura. His wife had taught him how to read. She'd been his own personal schoolmarm, and a particularly loving and patient one, at that. He hadn't spent a single hour of his childhood in a schoolhouse — he'd been too busy just trying to survive to worry about getting an education. Thanks to Laura, be could read and write. He had a lot to thank her for.

And, as his strength
Failed him at length,
He met a pilgrim shadow —
'Shadow,' said he,
'Where can it be —
This land of Eldorado?'

Lonaker lit a cheroot and was surprised to find his hands shaking slightly. He was as nervous as a boy about to steal his first kiss! How ironic, he mused bitterly, reproaching himself. Here he was, a man who'd spent a lifetime standing his ground against hostile Indians and ruthless badmen, and he was quaking in his boots at the prospect of facing a young woman!

'Over the Mountains
Of the Moon,
Down the Valley of the Shadow,
Ride, boldly ride,'
The shade replied,
'If you seek for Eldorado.'

In the lingering silence which followed, Lonaker heard the soft flutter of pages as a book was closed. Just as in times of danger, his senses were heightened.

Maybe I'm in more danger than I know, he thought.

"That will be all for today, children. I will see you back here Monday morning."

The children filed out of the schoolhouse in an orderly fashion. Lonaker counted fifteen pupils of greatly varying size and age. In twos and threes, or alone, they trailed down the road into town. All of them spared the troubleshooter a curious glance, but only one confronted him.

This was one of the older boys, a lanky and rawboned youngster. Brushing unruly black hair out of his eyes, he peered with stern suspicion at Lonaker.

"Who are you, mister?"

Lonaker smiled faintly, detecting an undertone of resentment "That's a risky question to ask on the frontier," he said, without rancor.

"I'm asking anyhow."

"William Endicott!"

Lonaker and the boy looked around.

Molly was standing in the schoolhouse doorway.

"You're asking any *way*," she corrected. "Though you should not be asking at all. The gentleman is quite right. Such a question is considered impolite out here. You should know better. Now go along."

The boy pressed his lips together, and Lonaker noticed his eyes kind of glazed over as he looked at the schoolteacher.

"You sure, Miss Kincade? This man's a stranger in Seven Springs, and I . . . and . . . well, I . . ." The blush started at his collar and climbed rapidly into his cheeks.

Molly smiled, then tried to repress it. "Thank you, Billy. I know you're only trying to look out for me, and I'm grateful, really I am." With a glance of quick appraisal at Lonaker, she added, "I'll be all right."

"Yes, ma'am. If you say so." With an injured air, and a sidelong scowl at Lonaker, Billy Endicott turned away and trudged down the road, glancing back with every couple of reluctant steps.

"I apologize for Billy," she said.

"No need. He's just worried I might be a gentleman caller."

"He's my knight in shining armor," said Molly, with a pensive smile. There wasn't a trace of sarcasm in the comment, but there was a dash of sadness. Lonaker was almost sure of it. "How may I help you?"

The photograph hadn't done her justice. She was even more beautiful. The tintype had failed to capture the natural grace which animated even her smallest gesture. Every move she made was a poem.

Lonaker decided it had been a mistake coming here. He could see that now. The last thing he wanted to do was hurt this woman.

Because he saw something else he hadn't seen in the photograph. Molly Kincade was lonely. He knew the signs as well as anyone. In fact, he was something of an authority on the subject.

And he was going to make it worse for her now. He was going to tell her that a man she had cared about was dead, and then she would be that much more alone.

"Is something the matter?" she asked, seeing the play of emotions on the strong features of his sundark face.

He had to say something. He was accustomed to going straight to the point. Now, as he tried for the first time to beat around the proverbial bush, he made a complete hash of it.

"I've . . . I've come about your uncle. Jim Sullivan."

"Oh!" Her hand flew to her throat. She knows, he thought. She can read me like a book.

"Well," she said, her voice trembling just a little, "I knew it was bound to happen." She looked away, across the sagebrush flat, at the town an arrow's flight away, at the river and the mountains beyond. Looking for something—consolation, maybe? And not finding it.

"Reckon I'll go," he said thickly, angry at himself for being such a coward. He hadn't had the guts to tell her straight out. So much for good impressions.

"No. Wait. Please." She bestowed a brave smile upon him, composing herself. "Do come inside out of this heat. Did you know my uncle?"

"Not really. But I believe he was a brave man who took the wrong road."

"So many of us do."

"Yes. I know."

"Are you going into town? If so, I wish you would walk with me. Tell me about my uncle. About . . ."

She bit her bottom lip, and tears glistened in her eyes. Lonaker felt sorry for her, wanted to comfort her. But he just stood there, at a loss for words.

"I'm sorry," she breathed. "I shouldn't impose on you. You may have important business."

"Not that important." Next to her, nothing seemed very important. "I'd be right honored to walk with you, ma'am."

"I'll get my things," she said, and disappeared into the schoolhouse.

Chapter Fifteen

Molly came back out of the schoolhouse with books tucked under her arm and smiled at Lonaker — a shy, surprised kind of smile, as though she hadn't really expected him to wait. As for Lonaker, his head told him to make tracks. He'd delivered his message, albeit in an inept way. But his heart wouldn't let him go. Strangely, he felt both miserable and elated.

She stood in front of him, waiting for him to turn for the road, and he just stood and stared at her. He didn't mean to stare, didn't want to, but he couldn't help it. She wore a simple brown serge dress, plain and functional, but on her it looked like the outfit of a queen. Lonaker had a hunch this woman could make a burlap sack look like the height of fashion.

"I'm ready," she said, a broad hint suggesting that it was about time they started walking.

"Yes ma'am," said Lonaker, feeling like a fool.

They proceeded down the road into Seven Springs, Lonaker leading the blazed sorrel. For a while neither spoke. It was Molly who eventually broke the silence.

"You're a lawman, aren't you?"

Lonaker smiled wryly, as though at a private joke. "Not exactly."

"Did you . . . ?" She faltered, drew herself up and inserted some iron into her voice. "Did you kill him?"

"No. But he was in my custody when he died."

"Your custody. Then you are a lawman."

"I am . . . was a troubleshooter for the Overland Mail Company."

"You aren't any longer?"

"It's a long story."

Part of him wanted to tell her the truth. Chances were better than fair that she would find out about his theft of the Army payroll, sooner or later, and he wanted her to understand his reasons. It mattered what she thought of him. This might be his only opportunity to tell her his side of the story.

But could he trust her? He wanted to. But wanting to and being able to were horses of an entirely different color. Objectively, he had to accept the fact that, conceivably, Molly Kincade was a Copperhead. And history was full of men who'd been led to their doom by a pretty face.

They walked on, and for a while no words passed between them. Lonaker could smell the faint fragrance of flowers in her hair, which the late afternoon sun streaked with highlights of gold and copper.

"They say my uncle was a bad man," she said. "A desperado. I suppose he was that. But he was always kind to me. Treated me as he would his own daughter. I was just a little girl when my parents died. Uncle Jim took me in. In those days he was trying to make a go of a farm in Missouri. Then my Aunt Ellie died,

107

and the crops failed two years in a row, and the bank foreclosed on him. Those setbacks turned him into a very bitter, broken man. But not so bitter and broken that he neglected me. He gave me all the money he could — sold everything he owned, except a horse and a gun. He found a place for me in a school for young ladies in Memphis, and then came West. We wrote to each other. I was the only family he had left, you see, and he was all I had, as well."

"I found one of your letters among his possessions." It occurred to Lonaker that to give the letter back to her would be the right thing to do. He had no business keeping it. As Alkali Jim's next-of-kin, she had a right to all the outlaw's effects. But he didn't want to part with the tintype. "I noticed you addressed it to James Kincade," he added.

"Aunt Ellie, his wife, was a Kincade. My father's sister. He thought it would be better if I didn't put his real name on the letters. He never tried to deceive me about what he was doing. He never lied to me. He promised me when I was a child that he wouldn't. I don't expect you to believe this, but his conscience bothered him. If you read the letters he wrote me you would know that to be true. He could scarcely abide the men with whom he rode. Despite what they say about him, I am convinced he never killed anyone, except in self-defense."

"I believe that," replied Lonaker. He remembered looking up the barrel of Sullivan's gun in Coyote Canyon. Alkali Jim had been talking when he should have been shooting. Lonaker wondered now if that had been due to reluctance on Sullivan's part to pull the trigger.

"You do?" asked Molly. "Really?"

Lonaker nodded, and her smile was so bright he had to look away.

"How did you get from a Memphis school for young ladies to a schoolhouse in Seven Springs?" he asked.

"I wanted to be as close to my uncle as possible. At first he was strongly opposed to the idea. He said the frontier was no place for a young lady alone."

"He was right about that."

"Do you think so? To tell the truth, I feel safer here than I ever did back East in the city. There may be some rough and dishonest men on the frontier, but they don't hold a candle to the seedy characters you find on city streets."

Lonaker thought back to his own youth, when he'd been forced to fight for survival on those same streets Molly was referring to.

"You have a point there, Miss Kincade," he conceded.

"And you have me at a disadvantage. You know my name, yet I don't know yours."

"Lonaker. John Lonaker."

"Well, Mr. Lonaker, if you want my opinion, the men out here have more respect for a woman, as a rule, than their Eastern counterparts. I suspect because there are so few of us. It's rather like gold—its rarity makes it valuable. Something to be cherished. I mean, what would gold be worth if you could pick up a handful off the ground everywhere you turned?"

"But women out here are rare, like gold. And men

109

fight and die over gold. They'll steal it, kill for it. Sell their souls for it."

She pulled up suddenly, and Lonaker took a couple of steps before realizing she was no longer at his side. He turned to face her, wondering if he had said something to upset or offend her.

"You're a cynic, Mr. Lonaker," she said, but a whimsical smile took the sting out of this rebuke.

"Or a realist, depending on your point of view."

She laughed softly, music to his ears. Like the song of a brook dancing down a mountainside — a sound tailor-made to uplift the spirit.

"Still," she said, "I feel perfectly safe out here. Most of the people are very nice to me. So many of them never had an opportunity to get an education, and above all they want their children to have that opportunity. It is so important. An education, I mean. It can make all the difference in life. You strike me as an educated man, Mr. Lonaker."

"My wife taught me to read and write."

"You're married."

He wasn't sure if it was a question or just a comment.

"I was. She's dead."

"I'm so sorry.

Quick to change the subject, Lonaker glanced at the books under her arm, and with a jolt of dismay realized how ungallant he had been. "Can I carry those for you?"

"*May* I . . ." She covered her mouth with a hand, her eyes wide with surprise and chagrin. "I'm sorry!" she gushed, contrite. "I'm so accustomed to correcting my students' grammar, I . . ." She laughed at herself.

Lonaker grinned. "I guess it shows I could use a little more educating. May I carry those books for you, Miss Kincade?"

She surrendered her burden. "Billy Endicott usually stays behind to carry them for me."

"I have a feeling young Mr. Endicott thinks I may be a rival for your attention."

"A schoolboy's crush, that's all."

"With such a pretty teacher, who can blame him?"

"Why, Mr. Lonaker! What a nice compliment."

The troubleshooter cleared his throat, acutely self-conscious. "I reckon every man in Seven Springs has a crush on you."

"Oh, I'm sure not." She wasn't being at all coquettish — her modesty was genuine.

"You made mention of a fellow named Dockery in your letter . . ."

"Simon Dockery. He runs a general store in town. He is one of my uncle's friends. It was Mr. Dockery, along with Mr. Endicott — Billy's father — and Mr. Sloane, who commissioned me to teach here. Uncle Jim put the notion in Mr. Dockery's head. I think he wanted me here so that Mr. Dockery could look out for me, as they say. He's a nice enough man, but lonely. A widower." She added the last comment as though it alone would suffice to explain the situation.

They were nearing the edge of town, and Lonaker caught himself dragging his heels. He didn't want this conversation to end. For just this little while — walking with Molly Kincade — he was able to lay his trou-

111

bles aside. She was nice, intelligent, easy to talk to. He'd forgotten how pleasant female companionship could be.

"Who killed my uncle, Mr. Lonaker?"

The question brought him crashing back to earth.

"A woman named Emily Venard, the wife of one of the Overland station agents. She was a Copperhead — a spy in the company."

"A Copperhead. You mean a secessionist?"

He nodded. "She killed him under orders. You see, your uncle was associated with a secret society called the Knights of the Golden Circle. Someone inside the Overland was informing him of gold and payroll shipments. The Copperheads killed him to keep him from exposing the informant. They . . ."

Her eyes were glistening with tears again. Lonaker shook his head, angry with himself. Not for the first time, he put himself in Sullivan's boots. Shackled, defenseless, experiencing the terror of knowing he was about to be murdered and unable to do anything to prevent it.

"He was in my custody," he said, bitterly. "I'm responsible."

"No you are not," she said firmly. "You didn't know, did you? About this woman, I mean."

"No."

"Then stop blaming yourself. My uncle ran with a dangerous crowd. He must have known the risks."

"You're really something, Miss Kincade."

She had the tears corraled, and the brave smile was back again.

They had reached the outermost scattering of

adobe and picket shacks. The road ran through the center of Seven Springs, terminating at the wharf where shallow-draft sternwheelers docked. No sand-river steamers were moored there at present. Two streets crossed the road, and at the first intersection Molly stopped.

"I live down this street. I'm boarding with an elderly couple, the Luticks. Wonderful people." She looked down the street a moment. Lonaker sensed she was struggling to make up her mind about something.

"I'll walk you down, if you like," he said.

"I don't wish to impose. I've taken up enough of your time. You don't know how much I appreciate your coming all this way to tell me about Uncle Jim. It was very kind of you. And difficult for you, as well. If only there was some way I could repay the kindness. I'd invite you to sit down to a home-cooked meal, but it wouldn't be proper, would it, to invite you into someone else's home?"

"I reckon not. But how about having dinner with me anyway? Seven Springs has a hash house, doesn't it?"

"The Riverside has a dining room. That's the hotel, down near the river, as you probably guessed by its name."

"So how about it? You can repay me by having dinner with me this evening."

She gave him a long, indecipherable look. Lonaker started to panic. What on earth was he doing, asking her to dine with him? What made him think she would be the least bit interested in having anything else to do with him? He was, after all, the man re-

113

sponsible for the death of her only kin. Besides, he hadn't come to Seven Springs to socialize.

"I'd like that very much, Mr. Lonaker."

He couldn't believe his ears. "You would?"

"Of course."

Well, I'll be damned, thought Lonaker. Now I'm really in trouble.

But Molly Kincade was the kind of trouble a man could stand a lot of.

Chapter Sixteen

"I guess I ought to walk you the rest of the way home," he said, "so I'll know where to find you later."

They turned down the street, past a few businesses — a barber shop, a laundry, a general store. The latter, Molly informed him, was Dockery's enterprise. An empty ore wagon trundled by. The driver tipped his hat to Molly. A pair of old codgers were passing the time playing checkers on a bench in front of the barber shop. They paused in their game to look admiringly at the schoolteacher and with brazen curiosity at Lonaker.

Their scrutiny gave the troubleshooter an uncomfortable feeling. He couldn't help but imagine that by now the whole world knew he'd stolen the Army payroll.

The Lutick place was an adobe house near the edge of town, shaded by several dusty alders, emcompassed by a low rock wall. Lonaker gave the books back to her, and they agreed he should come for her at sunset.

He took his leave, happy with the prospect of seeing her again, and yet troubled at the same time. Here he was, fighting for the life of the Overland—not to mention his own life—and he had the gall to ask a young lady out to dinner in the middle of it.

Lonaker shook his head. It was pure selfishness on his part. Molly Kincade was an addiction. She was all grace and mettle, and in his lifetime he'd met only one woman like her.

As he drew near Simon Dockery's general store, a thought struck him, and he quartered across the street. It was a spur-of-the-moment thing. He hitched his horse to a tie rail and stepped into the shebang.

The store was filled from floor to rafters with merchandise. Boots, longjohns, flannel shirts, dusters, hats, blankets, axes and picks and other tools, hardtwist and handguns, ammo and airtights, tobacco and sugar and other staples. The air was heavy with the aromas of leather and wool and coffee.

A man stood behind the dry goods counter, perusing a ledger. He was a husky man. His face was round and pale, like the moon. Thinning black hair was combed straight back and plastered with pomade. He wore a canvas apron over his clothes, and a pair of wire-rimmed spectacles on his nose. As Lonaker entered, the man glanced up, and the troubleshooter noted that the eyes behind the lenses of those see-betters were keen and cagey.

"Can I help you?"

"I'm looking for Simon Dockery."

The man peeled the spectacles off his ears and squinted guardedly at the troubleshooter.

"What for?"

"I thought he might be able to help me. Name's Lonaker."

"I know the name. Overland Mail Company."

"Until yesterday. I reckon you must be Dockery, then."

"I am. What do you mean, 'until yesterday'?"

"Let's just say I had a difference of opinion with Mr. Wells and Mr. Fargo. A political one."

Dockery slowly closed the ledger. Leaning forward on the counter, he clasped his hands, carefully lacing his fingers together. Lonaker's intuition told him that this man was plenty smart. Dockery knew what he was getting at. He didn't need it spelled out. The troubleshooter warned himself that to best this man in a battle of wits he would have to stay on his toes.

"Well, Mr. Lonaker," drawled the storekeeper, "I'm sorry to hear you're out of a job. But if this is your way of asking for a line of credit in my store, I'm afraid I'll have to know a little more about you. Such as what your intentions might be. I believe the Vallecito Lumber Company is looking for men. Or one of the mines hereabouts might take you on. I wouldn't recommend prospecting on your own."

"I'm no sourdough," replied Lonaker amiably. "No timberman, either." Quite casually, he swept the buckskin jacket aside and rested his hand on the ivory-handled butt of the Colt Dragoon riding in the left-side crossdraw holster. "I reckon I could use an ax or a pick if I had to, but this is the tool I feel most comfortable using."

Dockery's fleshy lips moved, the ghost of a smile. "So I've heard it said."

117

"And as there's a war coming, I figured I'd find plenty of work to suit me."

"I guess that's right. So you're headed east to join up?"

"I'd heard I wouldn't have to go so far to join up. There's a bunch calling themselves the Knights of the Golden Circle. Ever heard of them?"

Dockery straightened up, his eyes flicking to the door and then back to Lonaker. "Can't say that I have."

"Really?" Lonaker feigned surprise. "That's funny. I'd heard you knew about the Knights."

"Who told you so?"

"Alkali Jim Sullivan."

Dockery pursed his lips, stared at Lonaker from beneath bushy brows that came together as he frowned. Lonaker wondered if he'd gone too far, pressed too hard. He was a novice at this kind of deceit. But he gritted his teeth and played it out — maintained his poise, even though what he really wanted to do was dispense with the double-talk and drag Dockery over the counter and beat the truth out of him. He had to remind himself that the direct approach wouldn't work for him this time. For one thing, though he might be a shopkeeper and out of shape physically, Dockery struck the troubleshooter as a man with mental toughness. Not the kind who would give in to bare-knuckle intimidation.

"So you know Sullivan, do you?" asked Dockery, noncommittal in every respect.

"For a while. Before he died."

Dockery sniffed, hooked the specs back on his ears

and opened the ledger. He did not appear moved by the news of Sullivan's death.

"If you want to buy something," he said, without looking up, "it'll be cash on the barrelhead, Mr. Lonaker."

Lonaker grimaced. Either he'd scared Dockery off, or the man wasn't a secessionist after all.

"I thought you and Sullivan were friends," said the troubleshooter, grasping at straws.

"I knew him. I don't know that you could call us friends. He was, after all, a highwayman. And I am a law-abiding citizen."

"He asked you to look after his niece, Miss Kincade."

"You know a lot." Dockery nodded. "He did that, and it is a responsibility I take seriously."

Lonaker heard the door to the street open. Bootheels hammered the floor. Dockery looked past Lonaker. His eyes narrowed. The troubleshooter started to turn. The snicker of a gun being cocked, accompanied by a harsh warning, stopped him.

"Don't turn around. Hold your arms out away from your sides. Move real slow, Lonaker. Slow as molasses. Unless you want to take up permanent residence in the local bone orchard."

Lonaker did as he was told. He could tell by the voice that the man behind him was edgy. The troubleshooter was inclined to be very obedient with a nervous man pointing a pistol at his spine.

He kept his eyes on Dockery. The storekeeper stood with his hands on the counter in plain view, more curiosity than alarm in his expression. The possibility of violence did not appear to faze him.

Lonaker heard the other man step closer, felt the hard, cold reality of the gun pressed into the small of his back. The man reached around, yanked one of the Colt Dragoons out of its holster and hurled it. The revolver clattered on the floor and skidded away.

"Take it easy," said Lonaker testily. "These irons cost a lot of money."

"Shut up." The other Colt Dragoon was plucked from its holster. If anything, the man threw it away with even more vigor.

"You carryin' any hideouts?"

Lonaker shook his head. He thought about the collection of pocket pistols in the guncase of his custom-made Concord. Not bringing one or two along had been an oversight.

The man backed away. "Turn around, slow. Keep your arms held out."

Lonaker complied, turned to face a wiry man with sandy hair, muddy brown eyes and a thick mustache that completely concealed his mouth and drooped down below his jawline. He wore a blue broadcloth suit, thin kid gloves and a derby hat. Despite this attire, Lonaker sensed he was no dandy.

The man pulled Lonaker's saddlebags off his shoulder and threw them at the troubleshooter's feet. Then he held his coat open so that Lonaker could see the tin star pinned to his vest.

"I'm Flynn. Sheriff in this town."

Lonaker smiled. He was smiling, with bitter irony, at himself—his career as a desperado had been short-lived; apparently he wasn't cut out for it. But the smile made Flynn even more nervous.

"I know your reputation," said Flynn. "So I won't take any chances with you, Lonaker. You make one wrong move and I'll punch your ticket."

"Understood."

"Where's the money?"

"What money?"

"Don't muddy up my water," snapped Flynn. "I checked the saddlebags. I checked the blanket roll on your horse. You got it on you? Or have you already given it to Mr. Dockery? How about it, Dockery? You got the money?"

"What money?" asked the storekeeper.

Flynn's mustache twitched. Lonaker thought there might be a sneer under it.

"Mr. Lonaker here stole an Army payroll. Then he shows up in your store. Now maybe I'm just the son of a poor old Irish potato farmer, Dockery, but I'm not stupid. It's clear as mother's milk which side Lonaker is on."

"I don't know what you're talking about, Sheriff," said Dockery, with a righteous air.

Flynn snickered at that. "Sure. You're a damned secesh, Dockery, and we both know it."

"Have a care, Flynn," said Dockery, quietly indignant.

"I'll prove it someday," vowed the badge-toter. "Then I'll be coming for you. But today I'm here for Lonaker. Word come upriver from Yuma about your stealing that payroll, my friend. Then Billy Endicott tells me a stranger has shown up in town. I check out all the strangers that come into Seven Springs. To be

121

honest, I didn't think you'd be dumb enough to show your face in this territory after what you done. But you coming here makes sense, I guess. Plan to spend that money on guns for your bloody rebellion, don't you? It won't happen. Not if I can help it. I want that payroll, Lonaker."

Lonaker's mind was racing. If only he knew for certain where Dockery stood. Well, he had to play it through to the end based on the assumption that the storekeeper was a Copperhead. It was a long chance, but the only one he had.

"I buried it," he said, truculent. "You and your damned United States Army will never see a penny of it."

Flynn's laugh was a short, derisive bark. "We'll see. You'll have a lot of spare time in Yuma Prison to think twice about that."

Chapter Seventeen

At almost the same time Lonaker was tossed into the Seven Springs jail, Huck Odom was escorted from the Fort Yuma guardhouse to the office of Colonel Dahlgren. Huck was shackled hand and foot. This was the first time he had worn iron, and he didn't much care for it.

The four soldiers around him marched smartly in step across the parade ground, led by a young corporal who appeared to take his job very seriously. He set a pace that made it tough on Huck, who had to move along in a shuffling half-run, his stride constrained by twelve inches of stout chain which linked the hames on his ankles. On top of this, the reinsman was all but blinded by the blazing afternoon sun. Fort Yuma's brig was a windowless stone hut with a low-peaked roof of heavy-gauge tin, dark and hot and suffocating. The brightness of the sun was painful, but Huck was grateful for fresh air.

Colonel Dahlgren was seated behind a cluttered kneehole desk when Huck was brought before him.

"Take those irons off the prisoner, Corporal," he said.

While the guard worked with the stubborn locks, Huck stared dumbstruck at Sancho. The old *hombre del campo* was sitting in a chair beside the desk. He grinned affably at Huck.

"Bueno!" he exclaimed. "I am very happy to find you, Señor Huck."

"Goes double for me," said Huck fervently, rubbing wrists just freed from the burden of manacles. "It's good to see a friendly face. In fact, it's good to be alive." He glowered darkly at Dahlgren. "A man could die in that sweatbox of yours, Colonel."

Dahlgren was not visibly moved by Huck's animosity. "The Army does not mollycoddle its prisoners. When a man is consigned to the guardhouse he has done something wrong, and is to be punished for his misdeed."

"I haven't done anything wrong," said Huck coldly.

"So it would seem," conceded Fort Yuma's commanding officer. "The letter this man delivered absolves you of wrongdoing. Apparently." He added skeptical emphasis to the last word.

Huck took the envelope Dahlgren held out to him.

"This has my name on it," he remarked, "but it looks like someone beat me to it."

"I opened the letter. This man said Lonaker had given it to him to give to you. That being the case, I felt I was within my rights to determine if the letter provided information regarding the whereabouts of the stolen payroll. If you expect an apology, forget it. Corporal, you and the detail are dismissed."

The young noncom snapped to attention and led

the four troopers out of the office.

Huck opened the letter and read:

Huck,

I have reason to believe either McGrath, Raney or Coffman is the man we're after. Before he died, Fallon told me he thought one of the division agents had ordered Emily Venard to kill Sullivan. One of them is a Copperhead, committed to the destruction of the Overland Mail Company, thereby isolating California from the rest of the Union. I must find out which one, and the only way I can is by infiltrating the Knights of the Golden Circle.

The problem is that you can't be sure a man is who or what he appears to be in this business. I figure it can work both ways.

The secessionists are planning to take California, and the Territory, by force. I found and destroyed a cache of weapons and supplies in the Palomas Mountain. The Golden Circle will need funds to purchase more. I need the payroll to buy my way into the society.

I won't let the secessionists get their hands on the payroll if I can help it. As long as I am the only one who knows where it is, I will be more valuable to them alive than dead.

My actions will make trouble for you, and for that I am sorry. I hope you understand why I did not confide in you. This way, you are not an accessory. Hopefully this letter will be sufficient proof of that.

But use this letter to help yourself only if you

must. The fewer people who know the real reason I took the payroll, the better my chances will be.

If you can, get to Seven Springs as soon as possible. If I'm not there, wait. If anyone wants to know what you are doing, use your best judgment, but be careful what you say.

Your friend,
John

Dahlgren watched Huck closely while the reinsman read the letter, folded it, and put it back in the envelope.

"You look relieved, Mr. Odom," observed the colonel.

"I kept telling myself I'd hightail it out of the Territory quick as a duck on a june bug if John Lonaker ever went bad. Now it doesn't look as though I'll have to go."

"The fact remains, Lonaker stole an Army payroll."

" 'Diseases desperate grown by desperate appliance are relieved, or not at all,' " quoted Huck. "Shakespeare."

"Fight fire with fire, is what you're saying. Still, Lonaker had no right to jeopardize government money."

"Mr. Lonaker has always been the kind to do what has to be done." Huck pointed at the bullwhip coiled on the colonel's desk. "If you don't mind, I'd like to have that back."

Dahlgren gave permission with the wave of a hand. "So what do you intend to do?" he queried.

"I was about to ask you the same question, Colonel."

"Whatever I have to do to get the payroll back."

"Which means you'll need Mr. Lonaker alive. Give him a chance. If he can get into this Golden Circle and back out again, he might find out enough so that you can round up the whole lot."

"Or he could get himself killed. In which case, we'll never find the payroll." Dahlgren sounded like he had a bad taste in his mouth.

"He'll get out alive," said Huck. "I'm going to do all I can to help him."

Sancho stood up. "I will help, too."

"I'm still not completely convinced that this letter isn't some clever ploy," said Dahlgren.

"You know what your problem is, Colonel? You're too quick to believe the worst about people."

A familiar sound drew Huck's attention to a window looking out onto Fort Yuma's parade ground. He was astonished to see Betsy hove into view in front of the headquarter's building. The custom-made Concord came to a stop, and a moment later knuckles rapped on the office door.

"Enter," barked Dahlgren.

Sergeant Macready stepped in and snapped off a salute.

"Any problems with the Overland people, Sergeant?" asked the colonel.

"None I couldna handle, sir," grinned Macready, and winked broadly.

Dahlgren turned to Huck. "Your ride awaits, Mr. Odom."

Huck wasn't one to look a gift horse in the mouth.

He spun on his heel and headed for the door. "Let's roll, Sancho. We've got work to do."

"Mr. Odom." Dahlgren's voice cracked like a whip. "If you and Lonaker don't come back with the payroll, don't bother coming back at all."

"And don't go spreading what you learned by reading my letter, Colonel," countered Huck. "If the secessionists find out what Mr. Lonaker is up to, he's as good as dead."

"I'd be careful how you speak to the Colonel, me boyyo," warned Macready with a wolfish grin. His big hands, the knuckles cross-hatched with scars, closed into fists the size of sixteen-pound cannonballs. The three-striper clearly relished a donnybrook, and Huck's size did not deter him.

"At ease, Sergeant," rasped Dahlgren.

Huck and Sancho left. Macready was dejected. "You shouldna let a flamin' civilian talk to you that way, Colonel," he complained, sorely aggrieved.

"You'll get your fight," promised Dahlgren. "I want D Troop ready to ride in two hours. A week's provisions, and all the ammunition they can carry."

Unadulterated joy danced across the Irishman's craggy features.

"Yes, sir!"

"Sergeant, I have a hunch this is going to be more than a fight. It's going to be war. So try not to look so damned happy."

"Yes, sir." Macready endeavored to appear solemn as he left the office. But as soon as the door closed behind the three-striper, Colonel Dahlgren heard a lusty whoop of joy ring through the hallway beyond.

Chapter Eighteen

Night fell on Seven Springs and filled the cell block with shadows. Lonaker didn't mind the dark. It suited his mood. He lay stretched out on a narrow bunk in one of three cells in the back room of the jailhouse. A small window was set high in the exterior wall of foot-thick adobe. Through its four rusty iron bars, the Overland troubleshooter could see a strip of indigo blue sky striped with clouds. The sunset painted the clouds a vivid orange rimmed with gold.

Molly Kincade would be expecting him about now.

Though he tried to rein them in another direction, Lonaker's thoughts kept turning to Molly. He told himself he had a lot more to worry about. As Flynn had said, he faced a long stretch in the Yuma prison for the theft of the Army payroll, and he seriously doubted he could convince the judge who would preside over his trial that he had stolen the payroll with good intentions. A prison term in that Yuma hellhole was something to worry about, indeed. But Lonaker gave it hardly a passing thought.

What really worried him was Molly. Eventually she would reach the conclusion that he had stood her up. What would she think of him then? What would she think when she found out why? The more he brooded over this, the more miserable he became.

As the cell block darkened, he dozed. Her voice woke him with a start. At first he thought he'd been dreaming of her. Then he heard her again, and he knew he was wide awake. Molly Kincade was in Flynn's office.

She and the Seven Springs sheriff were talking. Lonaker couldn't make out the words. An inner wall of twelve-by-twelve timbers separated the office from the cell block, and the connecting door was closed.

The door swung open. Molly came through first, followed by Flynn, who struck a match and lighted a kerosene lantern hanging on a nail in the wall beside the door.

She wore the same outfit she'd been wearing in the photograph — kid-and-cloth shoes, a blue balmoral skirt, a cream-colored basque waist with delicate white lace at the throat. She approached the cell and looked at him through the bars, and he couldn't read her expression. Her eyes were very bright. He couldn't get over how beautiful she was. He stood in the middle of the cell, ill-at-ease, feeling ashamed, not knowing what to say. He thought perhaps he ought to apologize. But what he had done to her could not be set right by a mere apology.

"When you didn't come I decided to look for you," she said finally. "You weren't at the hotel, so I thought to ask Sheriff Flynn if he had seen you." She

130

looked down, and Lonaker realized it was difficult for a well-brought-up young lady to admit she'd gone looking for a man. She touched the cold iron of a bar and her fingers recoiled, as though they'd been burned.

"Mr. Lonaker will be staying at this hotel for a while," said Flynn smugly. "Until the circuit judge arrives. Then I guess you could visit him at the Territorial Prison, Miss Kincade. Though I can't imagine why you would want to."

"May we be alone?" she asked, with asperity.

Flynn gave her a long look. Then, without a word, he spun on his heel and retreated to the office, leaving the connecting door open.

"For some reason I just don't like that man," she whispered.

"He's just doing his job." Lonaker felt no enmity towards Flynn. The sheriff had guts and he was on the right side — violently opposed to the secessionists.

"He says you stole an Army payroll." Her eyes begged him to tell her it wasn't so. That it was all a big mistake.

"He's right," replied Lonaker, suffering a kind of anguish in his soul worse than any physical pain he had ever known.

"Well, you must have had your reasons," she said, her voice small. "The sheriff says you're a secessionist."

"I'm . . ." Lonaker cut himself short. He wanted to deny it, to tell her the truth. But would she believe the truth? Would anyone? He wasn't sure he would believe it, in their shoes. One thing was sure: he'd really

131

dug a hole for himself. That was a double-certified fact.

"Why did you come here?" he asked, more brusque than he intended to be.

She tilted her head a little to one side, narrowed her eyes. "I don't know."

He took the envelope containing the photograph and the letter she had written to her uncle from the pocket of his buckskin jacket, slipped it through the bars. "You should have this."

She took the envelope, glanced at the writing on the front, recognized it for what it was. Her puzzled eyes rose to Lonaker, but the troubleshooter had slipped back into the shadows in a corner of the cell.

"Good-bye, Miss Kincade," he said woodenly.

She turned for the door, and he could see she was hurt, and his resolve weakened.

"Just remember," he said, "that sometimes things aren't what they seem. People, either."

She paused in the doorway, listening, but she didn't look around, and when he was finished she slipped out of his sight.

A moment later Flynn stormed into the cellblock, his face flushed with anger.

"You bastard!" he snarled, the words dripping venom.

Lonaker lingered in the shadows, saying nothing. Flynn could scarcely make him out. The lamplight did not reach the corners of the cell. But he could see the troubleshooter's eyes, bright in the gloom like a cat's, catching and holding a glimmer of the lamplight.

"You're not worth a single one of her tears," rasped Flynn, and stalked back into his office.

Stunned, Lonaker stood there, his back pressed against the cool roughness of the adobe, for a long time. He watched the flame dance in the lamp's glass chimney. Way off in the night a dog was barking furiously.

I did the best thing for Molly. He had to keep reminding himself of that. She'd come looking for him. She'd cried. She was lonely, reaching out to him. But he had nothing to give her. It was better this way. Wrong time, wrong place. Lonaker had never felt worse.

Distant thunder intruded on his misery. He focused on the sound. No, not thunder. Horses. A lot of them, at the gallop.

His heart was pounding against his ribcage. They were coming for him. Somehow he knew it. Boots scuffed the hardpack of the alley on the other side of the wall. He glanced up at the window. A hand appeared, grabbing one of the rusty iron bars.

"Lonaker!" A fierce whisper — a voice he did not recognize. "Keep your head down."

Lonaker lunged for the celldoor, the thunder of the horses now loud in his ears. "Flynn!"

"What the hell . . ." growled the sheriff.

A volley of gunfire, crackling like heat lightning in the street, mingled with the shattering of window glass, the soft but deadly thud of bullets striking the walls. Hot lead whined through the open door into the cellblock, scarred the wall opposite Lonaker's cell. Slugs peppered the timber wall sepa-

133

rating the two rooms of the jailhouse.

Crouching, Lonaker watched Flynn stagger into sight, sag against the doorframe. His pistol slipped from twitching fingers. A bullet struck him in the back, hurled him forward. He sprawled in front of Lonaker's cell, knocking the lamp over, extinguishing the light, plunging the cellblock into darkness. He rolled over on his side with a guttural moan.

Lonaker heard wood splinter as the front door of the jailhouse cracked back on its hinges. Boots hammered the office floor. Lonaker stepped away from the cell door as three men entered the cellblock. Each man wore a duster and a hood with holes cut out for the eyes and mouth. Two were armed with pistols. The third carried a shotgun, which he broke open and reloaded as he moved. Lonaker heard more men in the other room — it sounded as if they were demolishing the office.

One of the hooded men knelt to rifle Flynn's pockets. He found an iron ring bearing a single skeleton key, and tossed it to a second man, who unlocked Lonaker's cell and threw the door open.

"Let's go."

This voice Lonaker recognized. He started breathing again.

"What kept you, Dockery?" he asked, pleased by how calm he sounded.

Dockery shrugged the crossdraw holsters bearing Lonaker's .44 Colt Dragoons off a shoulder, tossed them to the troubleshooter.

"Flynn's still alive," reported the man bending over the sheriff.

134

Dockery was already on his way out of the cellblock. "Finish him off."

The other man stood, straddling the wounded lawman, and aimed his pistol at Flynn's head.

"See you in hell," growled Flynn.

"Wait!" snapped Lonaker, struck by inspiration born of desperation. "I'll kill him. I want that pleasure for myself."

Dockery heard this and turned. For an instant frozen in time, no one in the cellblock moved. Gunfire crashed in the street. Dockery's hooded head moved in a curt nod.

"Make it quick, Lonaker. You two, come on!"

Lonaker stepped out of the cell, drawing one of the Colt Dragoons. He bent low over the sheriff.

"I'm on your side, Flynn," he whispered.

And fired.

He turned quickly away. The last hooded man was passing through the door to the street, into a night torn by muzzle flash. The office was wrecked. The desk and chairs and guncase smashed into kindling, the walls pockmarked with bulletholes. Lonaker crossed with long strides, paused on the boardwalk outside. A dozen horses milled in the street. The hooded men were mounted. One bent down to hand him the reins of the blazed sorrel. Lonaker holstered the revolver and swung into the saddle. A bullet whined past his head. Gun-flame lighted up the street, gun thunder bounced off the buildings.

Lonaker knew what was happening—the hooded riders had stirred up a hornet's nest. The good people of Seven Springs were fighting back, and giving as good as they got. Little did they know, mused Lonaker, that they were fighting their own neighbors.

The man who had handed him the reins cried out and swayed in the saddle. Lonaker reached out as though to steady him. The wounded man's horse jumped sideways as Lonaker grabbed a handful of duster and wrenched the man out of the saddle, let him drop to the ground.

"Let's get out of here!" yelled Dockery. "This way!" The hooded riders surged down the street. Lonaker followed, bent low in the saddle, running a gauntlet of gunfire.

Chapter Nineteen

As he fled Seven Springs with the hooded riders, Lonaker was feeling both gratified and guilty. Gratified because it seemed his scheme might work after all. These men were bound to be members of the Golden Circle, and he was riding with them. He wasn't too sure what they had planned for him, but it was a start.

The guilt came when he started thinking about the jailbreak. Had any innocent people been hurt or, God forbid, killed? The secessionists had burned up a lot of ammunition. Lonaker suspected they'd been trying to keep heads down, for the most part. If they'd hit anyone in the darkness it would have been by accident. Still, the possibility existed, and it nagged the Overland troubleshooter.

They kept their horses stretched out, running hard, for the first couple of miles. Lonaker realized they were holding to the road on which, earlier, he had met the old-timer in the supply wagon. The road, not much more than wagon tracks, curved up into the foothills of the Big Marias, and before long they were plunging into the woods.

No longer out in the open, bathed in the silver light of the early moon, they slowed their lathered mounts. The horses blew and whickered. Men coughed dust out of their throats. Some reloaded their guns. No one spoke. Grim men on grim business, mused Lonaker.

They stuck to the road for another mile, climbing steadily, and several times Lonaker glimpsed the lights of Silver Springs in the valley below through the tree-tops. A little further on they abandoned the road and descended into a deep draw, the horses picking their way gingerly down a steep, rock-strewn slope.

The draw was rimmed with mountain ash and juniper, clogged with thickets and fractured slabs of rock. Only patches of moonlight penetrated down into the bottom. Here Dockery finally called a halt.

"Fraley," said the storekeeper. "Shuck that hood and duster and ride back a ways. See if it's all clear. If you run into trouble, don't lead 'em back here. Fire a couple of shots and run for it."

The man named Fraley led his horse back up the side of the draw. Lonaker failed to get a look at his face. He wanted to learn the identities of as many of the Knights of the Golden Circle as he could.

Dockery dismounted, pulled off his hood, and walked over to Lonaker as the troubleshooter swung down and loosened the sorrel's cinch. "We'll wait here a spell."

Another man appeared at Dockery's shoulder. He was sharp-featured, with lank yellow hair and narrow, accusing eyes. When this one spoke, Lonaker recognized the voice. This man had been the one who had thrown the warning through the cell window just prior to the attack on the jail.

"I don't trust him, Mr. Dockery," he said. "He yelled out to Flynn right before you hit the jailhouse. Tried to warn him."

"Put the gun away, Johnson."

Lonaker had been concentrating on Johnson's face, committing it to memory, and at the same time checking it mentally against all the sketches of known hard cases contained in his "bible." No match. Now the troubleshooter looked down and saw a sliver of moonlight glance off the barrel of Johnson's pistol.

"I'm tellin' you, Mr. Dockery, he . . ."

"I gave you an order," said Dockery. His voice dropped a notch, but gained a measure of menace.

The gun was reluctantly holstered. Dockery turned to Lonaker.

"You weren't trying to warn the sheriff, were you, Lonaker?" The quiet menace was still there.

Lonaker forced a cold smile. "Why would I do that?"

"That's what I was wondering."

Lonaker's mind was racing. He knew he was going to have to come up with a plausible excuse if he expected to live to see the sunrise.

"I didn't know who you boys were, or what you were up to."

It wasn't much of an answer, but then he didn't have an answer. Somehow he had known, from the moment he'd heard the horses charging down the street, that these men were coming to break him out.

His calling to Flynn had been a slip. He'd been caught off guard. Everything had happened so quickly, and he'd shown his true colors. Now he was in a fix because of it.

Fact was, he and Flynn were on the same side. These men were the enemy. He admired the Seven Springs sheriff. These men, who did their dirty work in the dark of night with hoods over their heads, didn't hold a candle to Flynn.

Dockery was silent — an unconvinced silence. Lonaker played his last card, knowing that his life hung in the balance.

"Think about it, Dockery. I had no reason to warn Flynn. The bastard put me in an iron cage. Why would I warn a man and then turn around and kill him?"

This time Dockery had no answer. He nodded, glanced at Johnson. "Get back with the others."

Johnson did not look convinced, but he walked away without arguing the point.

"So what now?" asked Lonaker.

"You and I will wait here until first light. After Fraley comes back with the all-clear, most of the others will drift back into town. By ones and twos, once things have quieted down."

Lonaker looked past Dockery, at the dark, silent shapes of the nightriders skulking in the shadows.

"You see," continued Dockery, "most of them work in town. Johnson, for instance, is a barkeep. Fraley is a clerk at the hotel."

Honest citizens by day, thought Lonaker, rebel riders by night.

"You ride and shoot pretty well for a shopkeeper," he remarked.

"I fought in the Mexican War. Second Dragoons. Served under old 'Rough and Ready' Taylor at Resaca de la Palma and Buena Vista. Later, I worked for a freighting outfit and had my share of dust-ups with Apaches and border bandits."

"And now you ride for the Confederacy."

"That's right. We all fight for the Cause."

"Knights of the Golden Circle."

"For now. No uniforms. No flags flying or bugles blowing. We wage guerrilla warfare. Strike hard and fast, then vanish into the brush."

"You're in charge?"

"I'm in command of the men out of Seven Springs. But I take orders from Captain Lightfoot."

"Who is he?"

"Regular Confederate Army. Sent out from the East. I'll take you to him in the morning. He has a camp in these mountains. But the way is too dangerous to try in the dark."

Someone approached through the darkness. Lonaker was surprised to see it was Billy Endicott. Billy scowled at the troubleshooter before reporting to Dockery that one rider was missing, a man named Howell.

"He was shot out of the saddle," said Lonaker. "In front of the jail."

Dockery grimaced. "Was he dead?"

"I don't think so."

"That's not good."

"Joe Howell won't talk," said Billy.

141

"If you hadn't been so quick to put Flynn onto Lonaker none of this would have been necessary," was Dockery's stern response.

Endicott fumed. He dared not talk back to Dockery, so he turned his resentment on Lonaker, shaking a finger in the troubleshooter's face.

"You just stay clear of Miss Kincade, mister. You hear?"

Lonaker designed his smile to infuriate. He wasn't about to pass up an opportunity to sew a little discord in the ranks of the Golden Circle.

"You'd be better off not telling me what to do, boy."

Fists clenched, Endicott took a threatening step. Dockery lashed out and knocked him off-balance. Billy stumbled sideways.

"Get back with the others, Endicott."

Billy stood there a moment, glowering, legs splayed and head down, like a bull about to charge. Then he spun on his heel and stormed off down the draw.

"You could do with more men and fewer children," observed Lonaker.

"We make do with what we've got. I don't care how old they are. Billy will fight. They'll all fight for what they believe in. And we'll win, Lonaker."

Over my dead body, thought Lonaker.

He wondered how long he had before they found out Flynn was alive.

Chapter Twenty

Lonaker spent a restless night. He stretched out on the hard ground and tried to relax, with a rock for his pillow and a gnawing ache in his arm, courtesy of Fallon's bullet. He kept his hat pulled down over his face to conceal the fact that his eyes remained wide open and alert. The sorrel's reins were looped around his left wrist, and the cinch of his saddle was tightened up. If problems arose he could jump on his horse and try to escape under cover of darkness.

At least he had his Colt Dragoons. This was proof they had bought his yarn about stealing the Army payroll to help the Confederate cause. If escape was impossible, the least he could do would be to take a few rebels down with him.

The man named Fraley returned with word that they had not been pursued. Throughout the night, members of the Seven Springs chapter of the Golden Circle left the draw and headed back to town. Eventually only Lonaker and Dockery remained.

Lonaker's chief concern was that, once back in Seven Springs, one of the secessionists would discover

Flynn was still alive, return to the draw and warn Dockery, exposing Lonaker for the fraud that he was.

But maybe the sheriff wasn't alive. The troubleshooter was pretty sure Flynn had been hit at least twice by rebel gunfire. For his part, Lonaker had fired into the cellblock floor, but Flynn had already been seriously wounded — perhaps mortally so. At the time, volunteering to finish off the sheriff had been the only way Lonaker could come up with to save Flynn's life, but conceivably Flynn had been beyond salvation.

It turned out to be one of the longest nights Lonaker could recall, and he wondered if the dawn would ever come. But, as all things do, the night did finally end. As the eastern sky began to lighten, gray twilight slipped into the draw, and day broke with no one returning from town to unmask the Overland troubleshooter.

Dockery wasted no time in getting under way. They climbed out of the draw and gained the road, began to ascend higher and deeper into the Big Marias. They paused once, where the road clung to a wooded shoulder, at a spot where the valley below could be seen. Seven Springs was visible, but too far away to tell what was going on in the streets. The sun was just rising, and morning light turned the Colorado into a ribbon of gold. Woodsmoke escaping from dozens of chimneys wrapped the town in a blue haze.

"Won't folks wonder where you are?" asked Lonaker.

Dockery shook his head. "It's Saturday. Everybody knows I've got a little claim up here in the mountains.

144

I've established a routine of coming out every Saturday. Billy Endicott watches the store while I'm gone. I always get back in time for church on Sunday, and the people think I've been digging for the mother lode. The truth is, I report to Captain Lightfoot every week. I bring down his dispatches."

"Dispatches?"

"He keeps his superiors back east informed of the Golden Circle's activities, and he corresponds with local leaders like me. It's my job to see the dispatches sent on to their destinations. Most of them go downriver to Yuma on the mail packet. From there they go by Overland stage." Dockery chuckled at the irony of it. "Wonder what Mr. Wells and Mr. Fargo would say if they knew their express company was the society's line of communication?"

Lonaker didn't find it the least bit amusing, and he knew his bosses wouldn't either. But he forced a smile.

Leaving the road and the wooded slopes behind, they crossed remote mountain meadows guarded by crags and spires of bare salmon-red and buff-yellow stone. Bristlecone pines, isolated and ancient, clung tenaciously to fractures and ledges on the high, windswept rock. Saguaro and cholla towered above the scrub in the meadows, where clumps of hedgehog and prickly pear were blooming. Rockchucks whistled shrill alarm at their passing, and unseen diamondbacks rattled dire warnings. Flycatchers and woodpeckers were nesting in the saguaro, thrashers and shrikes in the cactus patches. An occasional eagle or turkey vulture soared high overhead, searching the ground for prey. Down in the thorny brush, swifts and horned toads darted away as the two riders approached, while up on the barren shale, gila monsters and whiptails slithered deeper into dark cool cracks and crevices.

Not much shy of midday, they arrived at the brink of a deep chasm. Here they dismounted to loosen cinches and give their mounts a rest. Curious, Lonaker eased as close as he dared to the brink of the canyon and looked over into blue shadow where the sun never intruded. He could hear the endless thunder of cataracts, could feel a cool damp mist rising from the depths, but he couldn't see the bottom.

"Watch your step," cautioned Dockery, squatting in the thin shade of a slanted boulder and sipping judiciously from his canteen. "That's Sidewinder Gorge. Empties into the Colorado a few miles south of Seven Springs. It's only three or four miles to the river as the crow flies, but the gorge twists and turns for at least ten to get there. That's how it got its name. You fall in, you won't get out till you reach the river. Of course, by then, you won't care. Wouldn't be enough left of you to drag out of the water. Indians say the gorge is haunted. I suppose it must be, 'cause the only men who ever went down there came out dead."

"How much further?"

"Not much. We'll follow the rim for about a mile and be there."

Their horses rested and watered, their own thirsts quenched, they pressed on. As Dockery had said, the trail ran along the rimrock, and in Lonaker's opinion it ran along too close for comfort most of the time.

146

Sometimes the way became so narrow that Lonaker's right-side stirrup scraped against a scarp of rock soaring skyward while his left-side stirrup dangled over a thousand-foot drop.

The roar of the torrent hurtling through the depths of the defile was loud in his ears—a deep and sullen roar which seemed to issue from the very bowels of the earth. In places where the sun had not yet reached, or never did, the trail was slick with moisture from the mist rising out of the chasm. When their horses started slipping they dismounted to lead the animals. On a ledge so narrow the simple act of dismounting became an adventure in itself, but Lonaker found he preferred being on foot. If the sorrel went over the edge he'd be sorry, but not as sorry as he would be if he went over with it.

The passage was not always so precarious. Where possible the trail veered away from the brink of the abyss, through brush-choked watercuts and over steeply sloped shoulders of mountains. Lonaker surmised that when it rained the watercuts quickly filled with freshets which in turn emptied into the gorge. When that happened, the trail would be rendered virtually impassable. Which led him to conclude that there had to be another way to reach the rebel camp. He asked Dockery if this was so.

"It's the only way you need to know about," replied Dockery.

Lonaker nodded to himself. Dockery might as well have come clean and said yes. There had to be another way. No hideout was worth using if it didn't have a back door. Probably a passage known only to a select few.

He decided it would be in his own best interests to find that back door. He planned to get in, find out as much as he could about the aspirations of Captain Lightfoot and the Knights of the Golden Circle and get the hell out while the getting was good. With luck he might discover the identity of the man he had started out to catch—the man inside the Overland Mail Company who had ordered the murder of Alkali Jim Sullivan.

But he reminded himself that escaping the clutches of the secessionists didn't solve all his problems. He was still, as far as the law was concerned, a wanted man—wanted for the robbery of the Army payroll. Would the law or the army even bother listening to him before they clapped him in irons or shot him down?

Still, you couldn't argue with success. The payroll was the only reason he'd gotten this far. And as for what the future held—well, he'd just have to cross one river at a time.

He was thinking they'd gone the mile Dockery had mentioned and then some when a man jumped down onto the trail from behind a jutting slab of rock and aimed a rifle at them. Dockery's horse snorted, jerked its head and began to fiddle-foot nervously. The store-keeper cursed in a strangled voice and checked the animal, trying to bring it under control before it danced right off the ledge and sent them both pinwheeling down into Sidewinder Gorge.

"Damn it, Skiles!" growled Dockery, breaking out into a cold sweat. "You're going to kill somebody

148

someday, you keep popping out of those rocks like a damned redskin."

Skiles laughed, pointed at Lonaker with the rifle. "Who's this?"

"He's with me," snapped Dockery, crossly. "I'm taking him in to see the captain."

Lonaker recognized Skiles. This man was a bona fide outlaw who had earned a page in the troubleshooter's "bible," a horse thief who'd killed a station agent while attempting to steal Overland stock. So these, mused Lonaker, were the kind of men the Confederacy was recruiting. Thieves, murderers and malcontents. Men who thought that fighting for the Cause would legitimize their lawlessness. Robbers and ruffians turned rebels. Lonaker didn't think the men from Seven Springs, men like Fraley the hotel clerk and Johnson the bartender, were much better. Just wolves in sheep's clothing.

"You can pass," said Skiles. He peered up the rocky slope above the ledge and waved his hat over his head in a slow, exaggerated, sweeping motion. Lonaker followed his gaze, saw nothing but sun-blistered sheets of stone spotted with boulders and clumps of cactus. He wondered how many rifles were up there.

"That's mighty kind of you," said Dockery sarcastically still shaken by the dangerous antics of his horse.

The trail curled around a shoulder, and then the ledge widened into a crescent-shaped shelf no more than fifty yards deep at its widest point. A dozen horses stood in a rope corral, lethargic in the furnace heat. Two men stood guard at the pyramid-shaped mouth of a cave. When Lonaker and Dockery appeared, one of the sentries stepped into the cave, emerging a moment later in the company of a third man. Lonaker knew in a glance this had to be Captain Lightfoot.

He was lean and lithe, of medium build, with aquiline features partially obscured by a close-cropped black beard. He wore his trousers tucked into high black boots, a short butternut-gray cavalry jacket, a hat with the brim rakishly tied up on one side. A pistol was stuck into a red sash around his waist, and a saber clanked against his leg.

"That's Lightfoot," Dockery told Lonaker. "Looks like a dandy, doesn't he? Acts like a real gentleman. But believe me, he's the last man on earth you'd want for an enemy."

Chapter Twenty-one

When Huck rolled into Seven Springs on the river road from Yuma he could sense immediately that something was wrong. So could Sancho, whose instincts were still, in spite of his years, as sharp as any man's.

The old Mexican rode in the box alongside Huck, even though Huck had suggested he would be more comfortable in the coach. But that was not his place, insisted Sancho. The coach was Señor Lonaker's home and he would not intrude.

So Sancho had ridden up top, not heeding the dust and the heat, and after a while Huck began to think Sancho could endure more heat and dust than he could. Something about the old *hombre del campo* made Huck glad to have him along. Sancho did not look very much like a fighter; he didn't even carry a gun or a knife. What he did carry was a bow and a quiver full of arrows. He told Huck he had made these weapons himself. He had learned how to do so from an Apache. The horn-backed bow was made of mulberry wood. The arrows were fashioned from carrizo reed, with hawk feather fletching. An old man with an old-fashioned weapon—yet somehow Huck knew he could count on Sancho.

There was definitely something wrong in Seven Springs, but exactly what wasn't immediately apparent. One clue was the way people watched them as they passed. Huck saw no children playing, and very few women on the streets. The men were sullen and jumpy, and most of them were packing iron.

When they rolled by the jailhouse Huck climbed the leathers and stopped the six-horse hitch. The front of the jail looked as though a regiment of riflemen had fired several volleys into it. Bullet holes pockmarked the walls. The windows had been shot out. Two men with rifles stood in the boardwalk shade.

"Looks like a good place to start," Huck told Sancho, wrapping the reins around the brake lever.

"*Cuidado,* Señor Huck," advised Sancho. "Those *hombres,* they hold their weapons too tightly."

Huck climbed down out of the box, debated a moment, then handed the bullwhip up to Sancho. "Maybe you better hold onto this for me."

He walked back to the jailhouse, nodded pleasantly at the men who blocked the bullet-splintered door. Sancho was right. These men were edgy, and they held their guns in the uncomfortable way of men unfamiliar with firearms. Which, decided Huck, made them especially dangerous.

"Afternoon," he said. "What happened here?"

"What makes it your business?"

Huck let the hostility run off him like water off a

duck's back. Lonaker's advice came to mind. He was walking on thin ice. He had to be careful what he said.

"I'm looking for somebody." A cautious comment designed to test the waters.

"You with the Overland?" The speaker was peering past Huck at the stagecoach in the street.

"That's right."

The two men exchanged glances.

"Look," said Huck, with an easygoing smile, "I'm not here to make trouble. I'm trying to find a man named John Lonaker."

They knew the name. Huck could tell by the way their eyes narrowed and their mouths stretched down at the corners that Lonaker wasn't going to win a popularity contest if these two were the only ones voting.

"You a friend of his?"

Common sense won out over loyalty. "He stole an Army payroll which was in the Overland's keeping. I want it back. Maybe I should talk to the sheriff."

The two men relaxed a little. "Sheriff Flynn's been shot up pretty bad," said one. "He may not pull through. Last night a gang of men broke Lonaker out of this here jail."

"Know who these men were?"

"One of them. We've got him locked up in here right now."

"Name's Howell," said the other. "Worked down at the livery."

"Damned secesh," grumbled the first man.

"Yeah. Who would have thought?"

This exchange gave Huck some insight into the situation. The bunch calling itself the Knights of the Golden Circle had broken Lonaker out of jail. Apparently the troubleshooter's scheme to infiltrate the secret society was working. The war had come to Seven Springs with a vengeance. These two — and probably a lot of other folks in town — were having a hard time coming to terms with that reality. The enemy was in their midst, and the enemy was faceless. No one knew who to trust.

"You think this man Howell might know where Lonaker is?" he asked.

"He's not talking."

"Yeah," said the second man. "Won't tell us who the other riders were, or where they come from, or where they went. Hell, they all could have been from right here in Seven Springs like Howell himself." He glanced at his colleague. "For all I know, Matt here could have been one of them." He tried to make it sound like a joke, and only halfway succeeded.

"That's not a damn bit funny," growled Matt. "I hear there's been talk of a lynching for Howell," he told Huck, and he didn't sound too opposed to the idea. He glanced nervously along the street, as though expecting to see a mob appear at any moment. Huck didn't think either man would go to any great lengths to protect their prisoner from a necktie social. "Maybe he'll talk when he feels the damn rope tickle his gullet."

"Watch your language, Matt," said the other. "Here comes Miss Kincade."

Huck turned, swept the hat off his head as Molly approached.

"You're with the Overland, aren't you?" she asked.

"Why, yes, ma'am."

She glanced at the two men guarding the jail, at their rifles. "Will you come with me, please?" she asked Huck.

"Yes, ma'am."

She led him at an angle across the street, on a course which took them near the Concord. Sancho raised his eyebrows in silent inquiry. Huck shrugged and motioned for him to stay put.

Molly didn't stop until they had reached the foot of a staircase clinging to the side of a two-story clapboard.

"Are you a friend of John Lonaker's?" she asked.

Huck started to give the same evasive answer he'd given the two men at the jailhouse. But something in the urgent, hopeful way she'd asked the question made him think twice.

"Yes," he said, chancing it.

Molly looked at him with such intensity that Huck thought she was seeing right down into his innermost soul. She was judging him, his sincerity, and in the end she judged him correctly.

"He's not one of them," she whispered. "He is not a secessionist."

"I know. Excuse me for asking, ma'am, but just how do you know?"

"I was the first person to reach the sheriff after those men broke your friend out of jail. I . . . we were supposed to have dinner last night. Mr. Lonaker and I. But the sheriff had arrested him. I went to see him, and I was only a little way down the street when the

155

riders came. When it was over I rushed back to the jail. The sheriff was badly hurt, but still conscious. He told me Mr. Lonaker had saved his life. He sounded surprised, like he couldn't believe it had happened."

"Saved his life? How?"

"Perhaps you should hear it from Sheriff Flynn. He is right upstairs, in the doctor's office. He's conscious. Dr. Mobley gave him laudanum before he cut the bullets out, but that was last night, and he came to a couple of hours ago. We heard the stagecoach. He said it might be someone with the Overland. He wants to talk to you."

Huck nodded, started up the staircase. Then he remembered his manners, stepped to one side and gestured for her to precede him.

"Sorry, ma'am. After you."

But she just stood there, gazing up at him, her hands clasped together, her eyes beseeching him for reassurance.

"He stole that payroll," she said. "I know that. But he . . . it wasn't for himself, was it?"

I'll be damned, thought Huck, flabbergasted. This woman really cared for Lonaker. Now just how had that happened? Lonaker had come to Seven Springs to wage a one-man campaign against the Knights of the Golden Circle, and yet he'd managed to capture this young lady's heart. No doubt about it, the man was full of surprises. Huck had to admit that working for John Lonaker was often dangerous, but never dull.

"No, it wasn't for himself," he said. "He's' out to

stop the Copperheads."

"Then we must help him."

"Yes, ma'am. We most certainly will."

Heartened, Molly climbed the stairs. Huck followed her into a cluttered office redolent with the smell of camphor, carbolic and alcohol. Two glass-fronted cabinets contained medical instruments and supplies. A bookcase was laden with big leather-bound journals.

"He's in the next room," said Molly, and led Huck across a threadbare rug, past a small kneehole desk covered with papers and more medical texts, into a second room just large enough to accommodate a red leather chair, a chest of drawers, a four poster bed and a small bedside table.

Flynn lay in the bed, the covers pulled up to his chin. His eyes were closed and sunken deep in their sockets. He was as white as a ghost. Huck thought he looked about as close to dead as a man could and still be above snakes.

"The doctor had to go see to Mrs. Weldon," explained Molly. "She's expecting. I volunteered to stay and watch Mr. Flynn."

Huck noticed she looked tired. Her clothes were wrinkled and spotted with blood. Flynn's blood, no doubt.

At the sound of her voice Flynn's eyes fluttered open. He seemed to have difficulty focusing on their faces.

"Is that you, Miss Kincade?"

"Yes." She went to him, felt of his forehead and turned to the bedside table, on which stood an enamel bowl filled with water. She dipped a cloth into the water, wrung it out, and dabbed at Flynn's cheeks and brow with it.

"Who is that with you?" asked Flynn.

"Name's Huck Odom," said the reinsman. "I work for the Overland. I've come to help John Lonaker."

A telltale floorboard creaked in the front room. Huck whirled to confront a bearded man wearing grimy leggings and a ragged serape. He had a patch over one eye, a scar on his cheek beneath the patch. Lost it in a knife duel, thought Huck, as he noticed the Arkansas Toothpick in a sheath on the man's hip. But it wasn't the twelve-inch gut-ripper that concerned Huck — it was the Remington Army Model the man was aiming at him.

"I've come for Lonaker, too," rasped the man. "But it ain't to help him."

Chapter Twenty-two

You'll have bounty hunters doggin' your heels, Dahlgren had said, hoping you'll lead them to Lonaker.

Huck realized this was precisely what had happened.

"Bounty hunter," said the reinsman, sourly.

"Ain't you smart," leered One Eye. "Dooley!"

A second man appeared behind One Eye. This one had sandy hair, a thick mustache, and the palest, coldest blue eyes Huck had ever seen. They were eyes that could send ice down the backbone of anyone they were fastened on. He wore a short buckskin jacket of Mexican make, and conchas studded his belt and hatband. Huck would have bet these two spent a lot of time down on the Bloody Border, slipping over to one side when they made things too hot for themselves on the other. Most bounty hunters were as bad as the men they hunted.

"I'm here," said Dooley. "All clear in the alley."

"Watch this big feller," said One Eye. He stepped wide around Huck to get a closer look at Flynn, and when he moved, Huck saw the short-barreled scat-tergun in Dooley's gloved hands. Dooley held the weapon loose and casual, but Huck wasn't fooled. In the blink of an eye Dooley could cut him clean in half.

"That ain't Lonaker!" rasped One Eye, scowling disappointment at the bedridden sheriff. He groped under the serape with his left hand and brandished a crumpled wanted poster. Shaking it open, he peered at the sketch, at Flynn, and finally at Huck. "What the hell is going on here?"

"Watch your mouth," said Flynn. "There's a lady present." His tone was fierce, but his voice was weak.

"And what are you gonna do if I don't?" challenged One Eye.

"Let her leave," said Huck, calm and reasonable.

"Don't think so," replied Dooley. "You look like the kind to do something stupid if all you got to lose is your own hide."

"Right," seconded One Eye, who couldn't disguise the fact that Huck's grizzly-bear size intimidated him. "You try somethin', the little lady might get hurt bad. Now, you was Lonaker's man, I hear. Tell me where he is."

"Mind if I see that paper?"

One Eye gave him the wanted poster. It shocked Huck to see Lonaker's likeness on the poster. Not a very good likeness, he thought, but good enough to get the troubleshooter killed. Nice work, Coffman. You're a big help.

"A thousand dollars, dead or alive," crowed One Eye. "Offered by your very own Overland Mail Company. Dooley and I aim to collect."

160

"John Lonaker will make short work of you," declared Flynn.

"Please, Sheriff," begged Molly.

"Yeah," growled Huck. "Keep quiet, Flynn." He had to admire the lawman's plucky spirit, but this was no time for baiting the bounty hunters. He handed the poster back to One Eye, who snatched it away. "I don't know where Lonaker is. I'm trying to find him myself."

One Eye glanced at his partner. "Damn it, Dooley," he muttered, as though Dooley had engineered this dilemma all by himself.

It was obvious to Huck that the bounty hunters had expected to find Lonaker in this room. Now One Eye wasn't sure what to do next.

"Let's dust out of here," suggested Dooley.

One Eye looked around the room. His gaze came to rest on Molly, and the corner of his mouth twitched.

"You're coming with us, darlin'."

Flynn made a guttural sound, tried to sit up and at the same time reach for the gunbelt hanging on one of the bed posters. One Eye swung his pistol around to aim it at the sheriff. The double-click of the hammer being cocked echoed loudly in Huck's ears.

"Try it, you're dead!" rasped One Eye.

"No!" cried Molly simultaneously. She stepped into the bounty hunter's line of fire as she tried to wrestle the gunbelt away from Flynn. Huck moved with astonishing quickness for one so big. He snatched the gunbelt out of both their grasps and tossed it away.

"Don't be a fool!" admonished Huck.

"We can't let them take her!" gasped Flynn.

161

"You'll get us all killed."

Dooley spoke up, his delivery flat, emotionless. "We just need her for a hostage to make sure we get out of this town. A lot of men are prowlin' around out there, and it seems like every last one of 'em is heeled. We were lucky to get in unseen."

"I'll go with you," said Molly, with a defiant lift of the chin. She glanced at Huck. "Don't worry. They won't harm me."

Huck wasn't so sure. "I admire your courage, ma'am. But I can't let you go."

"You don't have no choice," snarled One Eye.

Huck thought he did. He was betting that neither bounty hunter really wanted to start shooting unless it became absolutely unavoidable. They had sense enough to realize that with Seven Springs virtually an armed camp, gunfire would bring trigger-happy townsmen running.

"Maybe not," he replied, sounding almost apologetic. "Maybe I can't stop you. I wouldn't even try, were you to just turn around and walk away. But I can't stand by and let you take her. It wouldn't be right. It's a question of honor."

One Eye stared in disbelief. A slow, ugly grin twisted his scarred face. "Honor'll get you killed quick, mister."

Huck remained impassive as he stepped between Molly and One Eye. " 'A good death does honor to a whole life,' " he said. "Petrarch."

One Eye scowled. He threw a quick, perplexed look in Dooley's direction. "What the hell did he say?"

But Dooley was staring at the bloody tip of

the arrow protruding from his chest.

For an instant frozen in time nobody moved. Both One Eye and Huck were looking with paralyzing astonishment at Dooley, trying to make sense of what they were seeing. Dooley just stared at the arrow. Then his pale eyes glazed. The scattergun slipped from numb fingers and clattered on the floor. The bounty hunter swayed, lurched forward. His knees buckled and he fell on his face.

Molly screamed, seeing the fletched end of the arrow jutting out of the dead man's back.

Huck could see through the doorway where Dooley had been standing, across the outer office to the other door leading onto the staircase landing.

Sancho stood on the landing. He had already drawn another arrow from the quiver on his back, had it fitted to the bow and the bow drawn back. But he didn't have a shot at One Eye, who stepped back against the wall beside the door connecting the doctor's two rooms. Huck shouted a warning at Sancho as the bounty hunter fired around the corner of the doorway. The bullet punched the old Mexican backward. He struck the landing rail, which gave way with the loud crack of splintering wood, and Huck watched in horror as Sancho tumbled out of sight.

With an inarticulate roar the burly reinsman lunged at One Eye. The bounty hunter whirled, bringing his six-gun to bear. Huck batted the gun aside as it discharged. The bullet plowed into the floor. Huck threw a punch at One Eye's face, but the bounty hunter was quick. He dodged the blow and pistol-whipped Huck. Huck staggered, blinded by a flash of white light, stunned by the wicked impact of the barrel against his skull. One Eye lined up another shot, cursing foully at Huck. The reinsman threw himself at the bounty hunter's legs. One Eye fell, striking his gun-arm against the door frame and dropping the pistol as a result. He kicked Huck in the face. Huck rolled away, in a world of hurt. One Eye scrambled to his feet. He cast about for the Remington, couldn't locate it, gave up and made a dash for the door.

Spitting blood, Huck got up and went after him. To his surprise, One Eye didn't bother with the stairs. The railing on the side of the landing opposite the door had fallen with Sancho, clearing the way for the bounty hunter to launch himself from the landing in a flailing jump for the flat roof of the one-story adobe building adjacent to the clapboard housing Dr. Mobley's office. He landed, fell, rolled to his feet.

Huck didn't hesitate. He hurled himself through the air. His legs struck the edge of the roof, a painful blow to the shins that sent him sprawling. Getting to his feet, he saw One Eye draw the Arkansas Toothpick and drop into the stance of an experienced knife-fighter.

Huck crouched, circling warily, wishing he had his bullwhip. With it, he could have dispensed with One Eye and his vicious blade. As things stood, he found himself at a distinct disadvantage.

One Eye knew he had the upper hand. He laughed harshly, flipping the knife from one hand to the other. The sun flashed off the razor-sharp steel.

"I'm gonna cut your heart out, Overland man," leered the bounty hunter.

Huck spat another mouthful of blood. "Come and get it," he growled.

One Eye moved in, slashing laterally. Huck jumped backward. Again the bounty hunter lashed out, and again Huck managed somehow to elude the blade. The reinsman heard men shouting behind and below him and chanced a quick look over his shoulder. People were gathering in the street below, some gesturing at the rooftop. Huck was running out of room to maneuver. He tried to sidestep. One Eye cut him off.

"Where you gonna go now?" gloated the bounty hunter.

He lunged, slashing.

Huck thought about jumping. But if he did, One Eye might escape. And after what the bounty hunter had done to Sancho, Huck knew he couldn't allow that to happen. So he stepped into One Eye's onslaught, grabbing the bounty man's knife-arm above and below the elbow. With a mighty heave he hurled One Eye off the roof. One Eye yowled in terror. He struck the slanted boardwalk roof. The planks gave way with a rending crash, plunging him to the boardwalk. From the roofline, Huck watched him get ever-so-slowly to his feet. The man was one tough customer—Huck reluctantly gave him that. One Eye took a step, turned slowly and fell on his back. Then Huck saw the Arkansas Toothpick, buried to the hilt in the bounty hunter's chest. One Eye had fallen on his own knife.

Huck crossed the roof, jumped down into the alley where Sancho lay among the remnants of the landing

165

rail. As he knelt beside the old Mexican, he heard Molly rushing down the staircase, and was vaguely aware of a crowd forming where the alley emptied into the street. He was sick with regret, figuring Sancho was dead.

He was wrong. To his amazement, Sancho opened his eyes and smiled an embarrassed smile.

"I must be getting old," he said.

"My God, you're alive!" breathed Huck. "I was wondering what I was going to say to your wife and your children."

"Mi esposa!" exclaimed Sancho. *"Madre de Dios!* Do you think she would grieve? Do you think she would put on the mourning black? *Ojalá! Amigo,* I tell you, she would celebrate. I would not give her the satisfaction. She . . ."

Huck sat back on his heels and laughed until he could laugh no more.

Chapter Twenty-three

"The accommodations leave something to be desired," confessed Captain Lightfoot. "But please be seated, Mr. Lonaker. Make yourself comfortable." He gestured at a powder keg and settled on another. A gun case between them served as a table. A territorial map was spread out on the guncase, anchored on one side by a storm lantern and on the other by a revolver.

Lonaker sat, looked about him. They were in the cave, which had turned out to be quite large. At least as big and as high as a St. Louis cathedral the troubleshooter could remember wandering into as a child.

Most of the cave was being used to warehouse supplies and equipment — ten times what Lonaker had destroyed in the Palomas Mountains. The captain had his own private quarters set aside near the entrance. Two walls were canvas hanging from ropes. A third was gun crates stacked high. The fourth was the stone flank of the cave itself. In addition to the guncase table and powder-keg chairs, the area contained a field cot and a large trunk. Light was provided by the coal oil lantern on the guncase-table and another on top of the six-foot wall of crates.

"Not what you're accustomed to, I take it," said Lonaker.

Lightfoot shrugged. "I was born and raised on a plantation in Georgia, if that's what you mean. I'm here fighting for that home." He glanced at the young black man standing watchfully nearby. "Andrew, whiskey and two glasses."

"Yassuh." Andrew went to the trunk, returned with a bottle and a pair of shot glasses. He placed the glasses on the guncase, uncorked the bottle, and poured. He handed one glass to Lightfoot. Before he could hand the other to Lonaker, the troubleshooter reached over and got it himself. He didn't like to be waited on.

"Thanks, Andrew."

Surprise registered on the black man's strong features. He wasn't used to being thanked for services rendered.

Lightfoot said, "Unfortunately I have nothing better to offer you, sir. I brought two bottles of Napoleon brandy out with me. But that was a long time ago, and I fear the Napoleon brandy is but a sweet memory." He raised his glass. "To the Confederate States of America."

Lonaker raised his own glass in response to the toast and sipped the snakehead. Liquid fire trickled down his throat and exploded in his belly, reminding him that he hadn't eaten since yesterday morning—and that had been a frugal trail breakfast of hardtack and jerky.

Lightfoot downed his whiskey, set the empty glass

on the guncase. Andrew stepped forward with the bottle, but Lightfoot waved him away. The Confederate captain leaned forward, elbows on knees, hands clasped, and looked earnestly at Lonaker.

"Dockery tells me you've expressed sympathy for the Cause, Mr. Lonaker."

Lonaker nodded. Upon their arrival, Dockery and Lightfoot had spoken privately for almost an hour while the troubleshooter had waited outside. Following his conference with the captain, the Seven Springs storekeeper had started back for town. He would night in the mountains and arrive in time for Sunday services.

"He told me what happened in Seven Springs," continued Lightfoot. "I approved of the actions he took on his own initiative. We need more men like Simon Dockery. Men who can think. Men who can lead others."

"I'd say so," concurred Lonaker. "So far, all I've seen are hard cases and hotel clerks."

"A rabble now, I admit. But soon an army. A well-equipped army capable of bringing California into the Confederacy and seizing this territory. But that will be just the beginning. Ultimately, we intend to invade Mexico."

This revelation startled Lonaker. "You're joking," he said, and immediately regretted having spoken so carelessly.

Lightfoot's smooth voice was edged with steel. "You will find I do not joke about such things. We should have annexed Mexico fifteen years ago. We'd beaten their armies, occupied their capitol. Do you know why we didn't, Mr. Lonaker? Because Mexico would have become the most powerful slave state of all. And that was something the Northerners didn't want to see happen. So we gave most of the country back to them."

"I had no idea the Confederacy had designs on the Republic of Mexico," murmured Lonaker. It struck him as a grandiose scheme, an impossible dream. But with men as dedicated to the Cause as Lightfoot, maybe not so impossible after all.

"First things first, however," said Lightfoot. "As you saw, this cave is filled with arms and ammunition and other equipment essential to an army in the field."

"You must have a thousand rifle's here, Captain," said Lonaker, fishing for accurate information.

"More than that, sir. More than that. And we have a number of other, smaller, caches in strategic locations."

You have one less than you think, mused Lonaker, deriving secret satisfaction from having destroyed one of those caches.

"Still, we need more," continued Lightfoot. "Which is why your offer of the Army payroll is so welcome."

Lonaker finished off his whiskey. The ever-watchful Andrew stepped forward. The troubleshooter held out his glass and let Andrew refill it from the bottle. Again Lonaker thanked him.

"I don't recall having made such an offer," he told Lightfoot.

"Indeed? Mr. Dockery was under the impression

170

you had come to Seven Springs to enlist in the Cause. He assumed you meant to turn the payroll over to us." Lightfoot's frown was one of disapproval. "Why else would we have engaged in the risky enterprise of breaking you out of jail?"

Lonaker knew he was walking a tightrope, and would have to move with the utmost caution. One wrong step and he was dead.

"I guess I do owe you for that," he said. "I'm willing to share."

This didn't mollify Lightfoot. He brushed the territorial map aside, picked up a leather portfolio wrapped in waterproof oilskin. He brandished it in front of the Overland troubleshooter.

"Do you know what I have here, sir? Almost sixteen thousand names. The roll of the Golden Circle. Men from all walks of life, from San Francisco to Tucson, committed to the Cause."

"Your army," said Lonaker, eyes glued to the portfolio.

"Quite so. Men who believe in freedom of choice. Who are willing to fight against the oppression of a tyrannical government which tries to tell them what they can and cannot do."

Lightfoot spoke in a clipped, refined manner—he sounded almost English. The troubleshooter had a good idea of his background. Prominent Southern family. Plantations, tobacco and cotton, slaves, cotillions and fox hunts, the best schools. A man fighting to preserve his way of life. A gentleman who put great store in honor. An idealistic, intelligent Southern cavalier.

171

Yet Lonaker disliked him intensely. Lightfoot was worse than all the men in his would-be army put together. The troubleshooter could understand the outlaws who flocked to the rebel banner, lured by the promise of amnesty. He could even understand men like Fraley and Johnson—disaffected little men who wanted to be big men and thought their best chance would come in a new society of their own making.

But Lightfoot was a man who had everything, and just because his everything was built on the foundation of an institution—slavery—which was an affront to the very principles which had borne the nation, he was taking it upon himself to destroy that nation.

It struck Lonaker that Lightfoot had a lot of gall speaking of freedom and protesting oppression, with his slave standing not six feet away.

In Lonaker's opinion, men like Lightfoot were the ones to blame for this war. Their cause was corrupt. They misled their followers with catch phrases like "states' rights" and "free choice" when all they were really interested in was protecting their profits.

Lonaker glanced curiously at Andrew, wondering if Andrew recognized the irony of his master's comments. But the slave's features were as expressive as stone.

"These men," said Lightfoot, "are ready to sacrifice everything for the Cause, Mr. Lonaker. If you are not willing to do likewise, you have no place with us." He dropped the portfolio on the guncase-table.

Lonaker sipped his whiskey, his gaze drawn greedily to the portfolio. He couldn't believe Lightfoot was so careless that he would leave such an important document lying around. Then the troubleshooter remembered where he was, and how difficult it would be to get out alive if Lightfoot didn't want him to.

But if he could get his hands on that list, the Knights of the Golden Circle were finished. Lightfoot's army could be rounded up and locked away before they marched their first mile.

And the name of the informer in the Overland Mail Company — surely it was in that portfolio as well.

"All right," he said. "I'll hand the payroll over to you."

"Where is it?"

"I buried it. It's out in the desert, somewhere between Painted Rock and Seven Springs."

Lightfoot smiled tightly. "And you don't trust me enough to tell me where?"

"I'll take you to it. I'm going to be straight with you, Captain. I'll give you the payroll, and consider it an investment — in my future as well as the Confederacy's." He nodded at Andrew. "I don't own any slaves. I don't have a big plantation. I wasn't born and raised in a fancy house. I grew up in the gutters of St. Louis. I've risked my neck all my life just to make a few rich men richer. Now I want a piece of the pie. And it strikes me that pretty soon you're going to own the pie."

Lightfoot's expression was the barely tolerant one of a man who finds himself forced by circumstances to fraternize with inferiors. It irritated Lonaker, the way Lightfoot looked down his long, aristocratic nose at him.

"That payroll will buy you a rather large slice of the pie, Mr. Lonaker."

For all his poise and polish, this man, thought Lonaker, was as trustworthy as a rattlesnake. He was just the biggest snake in a hole full of snakes, and the most deadly of them all.

"I'll take your word for that, Captain," lied Lonaker.

Homer Raney pushed a corner of the canvas aside and stepped into Lightfoot's quarters.

"Actually, John," he said, "that payroll might just pay for the armaments you destroyed in the Palomas the other day."

Chapter Twenty-four

"Raney, what are you doing here?" asked Lightfoot.

Lonaker already knew the answer. Raney was pointing a gun at him. That in itself spoke volumes. The small, round-shouldered man was his usual quiet, businesslike self. He displayed no anger or excitement. No posturing or shouting. The expression on his bloodhound features was as doleful as ever. But Lonaker didn't doubt that Homer Raney would shoot if he made one wrong move. And, as in all things, he would be very efficient.

"I thought you ought to know what happened with Sullivan and the payroll we were after," replied Raney.

"Mr. Lonaker stole the payroll."

"Did he? I wonder."

Lightfoot looked with cold scrutiny at the Overland troubleshooter.

"Homer, you surprise me," said Lonaker, with the sublime calm of an innocent man. "I had no idea you were on the side of the Confederacy."

"You're a slick one, John. You must have ice in your veins."

Lightfoot stood up. "What exactly is going on here, Raney?"

"John dispensed with Sullivan's gang of cutthroats and captured Alkali Jim himself. I was afraid Sullivan would expose me, so I ordered Emily Venard to kill him. She did, and John killed her. I also sent Fallon to notify you. I told him he could swing by the Palomas cache, since it was on the way, for provisions and a saddle. That's where I made my mistake. I didn't think John would go after him." He turned to Lonaker. "I thought you'd stick with the payroll, see it safely to Fort Yuma."

"Fallon never came to me," said Lightfoot.

"No, because John tracked him to the Palomas hideout and killed him. I tell you, John, you've done some damage. Sullivan's gang, Emily, Fallon. Worst of all, Captain, he destroyed the supplies we had stored in the Palomas. Every last Enfield and round of ammunition, up in smoke."

Lightfoot glared at Lonaker. "Is this true?"

"Of course not."

"No point in denying it, John," said Raney, sounding almost apologetic. "You're caught. I started worrying when you went after Fallon. Worried about it all the rest of that day, while riding the eastbound stage with McGrath. That night we stopped at the Medicine Flats station. When everyone was asleep I took a horse and made for the Palomas. Took me almost two days. I found Fallon dead, and the stores destroyed, and empty shell casings from your Henry rimfire. That brand new repeating rifle of yours leaves a distinctive trail all its own, John."

176

Lonaker tried to read Captain Lightfoot and gauge his chances of talking his way out of this fix. He watched the last glimmer of uncertainty fade from the Confederate officer's face. Lightfoot took a step back from the guncase-table. That, decided Lonaker, was a bad sign. A man didn't want to stand too close to the enemy. Lightfoot reached across his body with his right hand and grasped the single-guard hilt of the saber at his side.

"Stand up, John," said Raney. "Unbuckle those gunbelts and let them drop, nice and easy."

"Don't kill him yet," ordered Lightfoot. "I want to know where that payroll is buried."

Raney shook his head. "You don't know this man as well as I do, Captain. You are mistaken if you think you can force him to talk."

"I'll take that as a compliment," said Lonaker.

"It's too bad, really," said Raney. "The Cause could use men like you, John."

"You and your damned Cause can go straight to hell, Homer."

Andrew, standing behind Raney, raised the bottle of red-eye and brought it down hard on the division agent's skull.

Raney folded, collapsing in a shower of whiskey and broken glass.

The whisper of steel accompanied Lightfoot's act of drawing the saber. Lonaker jumped up with both Colt Dragoons drawn before the Confederate captain could get the saber half-clear of its scabbard.

"Ready to die, Captain?"

Lightfoot froze. He gazed with cold disdain at Lonaker.

"You have me at a disadvantage, sir," he said stiffly.

"What do you want? Pistols at twenty paces? Forget it. I'm no gentleman, and I don't fight fair."

"This is readily apparent." Lightfoot transferred his frosty glare to Andrew. "You will live to regret this, boy."

Standing over the unconscious Raney, still clutching the jagged neck of the whiskey bottle in a white-knuckled stranglehold, Andrew was as inscrutable as ever.

"Yassuh, mos' likely Ah will. Ah done lived to regret a whole lotta things already. Like de day I was born. And de day you sol' my pappa. And de night you took my sister. And ever' scar on my back from dat overseer's whip."

Lightfoot stared as though he didn't understand a word.

"Get rid of the saber, Captain," said Lonaker.

Lightfoot unbuckled the swordbelt and tossed the weapon onto the field cot. He stood stiffly erect, as though at attention. Lonaker holstered one of the Colt Dragoons and picked up the leather portfolio containing the names of sixteen thousand secessionists.

"You won't get out of here alive," said Lightfoot.

"You're going to take me out." The troubleshooter stuffed the portfolio under his shirt.

Lightfoot's expression was one of withering contempt, his smile wintery.

"You are gravely mistaken, sir."

178

He lunged for the pistol on the guncase. The move surprised Lonaker, for the simple reason that it was a suicide play. Lightfoot didn't stand a chance, and the thought flashed through Lonaker's mind that he'd misjudged this Southern cavalier. The man was ready to die for his beloved Cause.

Lonaker could have shot him down. Instead, he used the Colt Dragoon to club Lightfoot. As soon as the first shot was fired, Lightfoot's men would come running. Lonaker's problem was that he wasn't sure how many men Lightfoot had here in this secret mountain camp. He'd seen two at the cave's entrance, a few more among the stores deeper in the cave, and one on the trail. But there had been more hidden up on the slope, and probably more than he had seen in the cave itself.

The gun barrel struck Lightfoot's head a glancing blow. He fell sideways, but he took the pistol with him. Lonaker cursed under his breath. He had no choice now.

He fired a fraction of a second before Lightfoot. His bullet hit home. Lightfoot's went wide, whining off rock. A blue hole suddenly appeared in the Confederate's forehead. His body went rigid for an instant. Then he flopped backward and lay sprawled at Andrew's bare feet. Stunned, Andrew stared at the corpse that was staring up at him with hooded, sightless eyes.

Men shouted from deeper in the cave. Lonaker stepped toward Andrew, border rolled the Colt Dragoon and offered it butt-first.

"Can you shoot?"

179

"Ah reckon." Andrew gingerly took the gun.

"I appreciate what you did." Lonaker nodded at the unconscious Raney. "I'll kill this man right here and now, and you can stay put. No one but me will know what happened. Maybe you'll be able to slip away in the confusion."

"You'd kill this here man in cold blood, for me?"

"If I have to."

Andrew pursed his lips, thought it over, and shook his head morosely.

"Nossuh, Ah reckon not. Ah done come dis far. Only thing to do's see it through to de end."

Lonaker nodded. "You're a good man, Andrew. I'm glad you're on my side."

"Ah reckon it's you what's on my side, suh, when it comes down to it."

Lonaker drew the other Colt Dragoon. "Is there another way out besides the way I came in?"

"Yassuh. In de back of dis here cave, a tunnel."

"Let's try for it."

Chapter Twenty-five

Lonaker moved to the corner where the two canvas walls met and pushed through. He collided with a running man. The man had his gun drawn, but he wasn't quick enough to save himself. Lonaker knocked him backward with an elbow in the face and fired. The bullet drove the man to the ground. Lonaker spared him only a glance. He looked vaguely familiar. If I can wipe out this nest of two-legged vipers, he thought, I could tear a lot of pages out of my bible.

Bullets burned the air around him. Gunfire thundered in the confines of the cave. Lonaker spotted four men working their way forward from the rear of the cave, moving cautiously through the stacks of crates and kegs. The two men on sentry duty at the entrance were closing in from the other direction. Lonaker and Andrew were caught in a blistering crossfire. The troubleshooter whirled and fired two shots at the four men darting among the stores. Andrew followed suit. The Copperheads ducked behind cover.

Lonaker made his break for the cave entrance, discarding the notion of escape through the tunnel Andrew had mentioned. It was simple ciphering. There were four men to get by in that direction, and only two at the mouth of the cave. If they could get past those two and reach the horses, maybe they would make it.

Seeing Lonaker and Andrew turn toward them, the two guards pulled up. One knelt, the other remained standing, and both were shooting as fast as they could. But they were using breech-loading rifles, not repeaters. The new repeating rifles were still hard to come by, and Lonaker counted his blessings in that respect. He emptied his pistol, always moving, and his last shot dropped one of the guards. At the same moment Andrew uttered a strangled cry and fell, a bullet smashing into his spine, fired by one of the men further back in the cave. He died instantly.

Lonaker didn't have time to feel sorry about Andrew. He holstered the empty Colt Dragoon and bent to retrieve the gun Andrew had dropped. Not knowing if the revolver was empty or not, he aimed the gun at the second guard and pulled the trigger. The guard sprawled, gut-shot. A bullet tugged at Lonaker's buckskin jacket. He rolled and came up shooting back into the cave. The Colt Dragoon barked twice more. Then the hammer fell on an empty chamber.

The troubleshooter ran for it. The secret was to keep moving. He'd learned that lesson from Plains Indians. Out on the prairie there wasn't a lot of cover, so the best thing to do in a fight was to make yourself a target that was hard to hit. You never saw a Sioux or

Cheyenne warrior rooted in one place too long in a fracas.

He burst out of the cave at full speed, out into the open of the mountainside shelf. The Copperheads up in the rocks were waiting for something to shoot at. Several rifles spoke at once. Bullets peppered the ground on all sides of Lonaker.

But his luck was holding. The day was nearing its end. The sun had dropped behind the rugged heights of the Big Marias, and beneath a purple sky the gorge was steeped in indigo shadows which made accurate long-range shooting difficult.

Lonaker sprinted for the rope corral. The blazed sorrel was tethered to one of the ropes strung between iron stakes. It was still saddled. More good fortune. The troubleshooter wondered when his luck would run out.

Reaching the horse, he drew the Henry from the saddle boot. Scanning the slopes, he could see nothing of the enemy except muzzle flash and white puffs of gunsmoke. He fired five rounds at their positions as fast as he could work the rifle's action. All he hoped to do was keep their heads down.

He freed the reins and vaulted into the saddle. The four men were coming out of the cave now. Lonaker fired the Henry one-handed. Wedging the barrel between his leg and the saddle fender, he worked the action and fired again. He sawed the reins with his left hand to keep the prancing sorrel under control. One of the Copperheads fell, clutching his leg. The other three dived back into the cave. The wounded man crawled after them. Lonaker gave no thought to finishing him off. He had to get out of this hot-lead hail-storm.

Wheeling the horse around, he kicked it into a canter. As they neared the brink of Sidewinder Gorge the sorrel's nostrils flared at the cool damp mist rising from the dark depths, laid its ears back against the ominous roar of raging torrents. Fighting against the bit in its mouth, the horse balked. Lonaker cursed, slapped the still-hot barrel of the Henry against the sorrel's haunch. The animal succumbed to its riders wishes, allowed Lonaker to turn it onto the ledge. It settled into a nervous trot and protested when Lonaker tried to lash a faster gait out of it.

The troubleshooter turned his attention to the steep mountainside looming above him. He saw several men, indistinct shapes darting from boulder to cactus clump to rock pile in crouching runs. They fired downslope now and then, but the task of keeping their footing on the treacherous incline was a distraction which worked to Lonaker's benefit. They were making their way down the slope at an angle, trying to keep abreast of him. Lonaker fired back a few times, knowing how unlikely it would be to hit anyone, hoping only to slow them down.

The sorrel was bound and determined to take the ledge in its own good time, so Lonaker's flight was not as rapid as he desired. Still, he was encouraged. That he had gotten this far was nothing short of miraculous. He was beginning to think he might actually get away when the man named Skiles dropped down from behind an outcropping of rock onto the ledge right in front of him.

Before Lonaker could bring the Henry to bear, Skiles fired his own rifle from hip level. Startled by the man's sudden appearance, the sorrel jerked its head up. The bullet smashed into its throat. The animal's front legs buckled. Lonaker kicked out of the stirrups and was thrown forward as the horse dropped dead in its tracks.

The fall jarred the repeater out of his grasp. He struck his head on stone and almost passed out. To make matters worse, he took the brunt of the fall on his left side. The recent gunshot wound in his left shoulder sent bolts of pain shooting through his entire body.

Half-blinded by dancing pinpricks of white light, Lonaker looked up to see Skiles moving toward him. The man was thumbing another load into the breech of his single-shot long gun. The Overland troubleshooter felt a cold hard knot twist in his belly as he realized the Colt revolvers in his crossdraw holsters were empty and that he'd lost the Henry. He threw a quick look around, didn't see the rifle, and wasted no more time in the search. Blocking out the pain, refusing to give in to weakness, he surged to his feet and hurled himself at Skiles.

The look of surprise on the outlaw's face revealed that he had underestimated Lonaker's resilience—deemed the troubleshooter too hurt to offer further resistance, and was getting closer for a certain shot, a bullet in the brainpan. This faulty reckoning cost him dearly.

He tried to bring the rifle to bear, but Lonaker struck it away as he plowed into the outlaw-turned-

185

rebel. They fell, grappling, punching. Skiles lost his grip on the breech-loader. He kneed Lonaker in the groin, driving the breath out of the troubleshooter. Skiles was strong and wiry, a vicious fighter. Still shaken by his fall, wracked with pain, Lonaker was at a disadvantage.

The outlaw's rock-hard fist slammed into the side of Lonaker's head. Ears ringing, the troubleshooter rolled away. Skiles bounced to his feet and groped for the six-gun on his hip. Lonaker felt a stone beneath his hand. He picked it up and threw it as hard as he could. The rock, striking Skiles squarely in the jaw, staggered him. Lonaker heaved himself up and slammed into Skiles again, throwing a flurry of punches. Skiles sagged to his knees, blood streaming from nose and mouth. He raised the pistol. Lonaker kicked it away. Skiles clutched at Lonaker's legs and brought the troubleshooter down. They rolled across the ledge — and right to the rim of the gorge.

Lonaker sensed rather than saw this. He stopped fighting and tried to break free of Skiles, struggling with new strength born of desperation. But Skiles was already slipping over the edge. His legs flailed at empty space. He clung to Lonaker for all he was worth. Lonaker felt himself being dragged over the brink by the outlaw's weight. He clawed at the ledge until his hands were raw and bleeding. At the same time he tried to kick Skiles loose.

But Skiles was hanging on, literally, for dear life. His breath came in short, quick, terrified gasps. He grabbed hold of one of Lonaker's gunbelts and hooked the other arm around Lonaker's legs. He was all the way off the ledge now, and he was taking Lonaker with him.

Then Lonaker's hand brushed leather — the sorrel's reins. He clutched the reins with both hands. He was anchored to the ledge now by half a ton of dead horse. If he could only hold on. If only the bridle wouldn't break under the combined weight of two men.

Clinging to the strips of leather with his right hand, he swung his left fist down into Skiles's face. Skiles cried out — a guttural cry of sheer terror — as he lost his grip on Lonaker's gunbelt. Lonaker struck again and again. Each blow sent waves of nauseating pain rolling through him. And with each blow Skiles slipped further down the troubleshooter's legs. He couldn't defend himself.

Lonaker felt the reins slip through his right hand, burning the flesh of his palm. He couldn't hold on much longer. He could no longer reach the outlaw's bloodied face. But he got his fingers tangled in Skiles's hair and yanked with all his strength, pulling until the pain from his wound made him snarl like a wild animal caught in a trap. The snarl mingled with the outlaw's shriek of helpless rage. His hold on Lonaker's legs loosened. The troubleshooter pulled one leg free and brought it down savagely into Skiles's face. The heel of his boot crushed the man's nose. With one last strangled cry, Skiles lost his grip and fell.

Lonaker hauled himself back onto the ledge, grunting with the exertion. He lay there a moment, the breath rasping in his throat. Somewhere on the slope above him a man shouted. A small avalanche of rocks pelted the ledge and stirred him. He pushed wearily up onto shaky legs and broke into a shambling run along the ledge.

He looked back a few times, peering into the deepening shadows of the fast-coming night, saw no one, and kept running. Fumbling with stiff, bloody, trembling fingers to load one of his revolvers while he ran, he felt the portfolio beneath his shirt, its oilskin wrapping clinging to the cold sweat on his skin.

Chapter Twenty-six

"Lonaker saved my life," said Flynn. "No two ways about it. Thing is, until the last second, when he turned the gun away from my head and fired into the floor, I thought he was going to kill me."

Huck stood despondently at the window, looking down into the street. The last light of day had bled slowly out of the sky, and the warm buttery yellow of lamplight shone in other windows from one end of Seven Springs to the other. The town was quiet now. It was suppertime. Most of the folks were sitting down to table. Huck's stomach growled, reminding him he needed some vittles.

If he put his face close to the glass and looked up the street he could just see the jailhouse, and the dark shapes of the guards in the blue-black shadow beneath the boardwalk awning.

The bodies of the two bounty hunters were now in the care and keeping of the town's undertaker, being measured for their coffins. In the morning they would take up permanent residence in the local boot hill, occupants of nameless graves, soon to be forgotten.

But Huck didn't think he would ever forget. He'd killed a man. Not his first. But it didn't get any easier for him. It didn't make any difference that One Eye had been a bad character. Nor did it matter that the bounty hunter had fallen on his own knife. Huck had killed him and there was no way around it.

At least One Eye and his partner in manhunting would get decent burials. Would John Lonaker? Huck's brooding gaze rose to the moon-silvered peaks of the Big Marias. Or was the troubleshooter dead, scavenger meat on some rocky mountainside?

Such was Huck Odom's dilemma. He wanted to help Lonaker, assuming Lonaker wasn't already beyond help. But he didn't know where or how to find the Overland troubleshooter.

"Get to Seven Springs as soon as possible," Lonaker had written. "If I'm not there, wait." Well, waiting was just not Huck's cup of tea. He was restless, edgy — a state of mind demonstrated by the way he jumped when the door to Doc Mobley's outer office opened and the sawbones stuck his head into the room.

"Your friend is resting quietly," he informed Huck. "I got the bullet out of his shoulder. No broken bones, which I find pretty remarkable, considering the fall."

"Sancho is a tough bean."

Mobley nodded. He was a middle-aged man, pale and haggard, with moist brown eyes so dark they seemed black. He looked tired and sad and wise. Huck had a hunch Mobley always looked this way. When he smiled it was halfheartedly, as though he knew that anything in this world that could make a

190

man smile didn't last long. It had something to do, Huck figured, with all the pain and suffering the man had witnessed during years of heartbreaking struggle against death and disease.

"I know he is," said Mobley. "He refused laudanum or whiskey before I took the knife to him. He said he'd chew peyote if I had any. Of course I didn't. He didn't make a sound as I probed for the bullet. Didn't even twitch. I complimented him on his ability to withstand pain. He said I didn't know anything about pain unless I'd met his wife."

"He does tend to carry on about the woman."

"Well, like I said, he's resting quietly. He needs to stay in bed for a few days at least. A week would be better. Two weeks would be too much to hope for with such a man. Miss Kincade is with him now." Mobley glanced at Flynn. "How are you doing, Sheriff?"

"Good, Doc. Good."

"Don't wear yourself out. You need rest, and lots of it." Mobley threw a significant glance at Huck.

"Just a few more minutes, Doc," promised the reinsman. He wanted to find out what Flynn knew and then pay Sancho a visit. The old Mexican had been put up in the hotel down by the river.

Mobley nodded and closed the door.

"What are you going to do?" asked Flynn.

"I wish I knew."

"The men who attacked the jail all wore hoods. But I know who two of them were."

Two long strides brought Huck to the bedridden sheriff's side. Flynn had slipped into unconsciousness after the confrontation with One Eye and Dooley.

191

When Huck had gone after One Eye, Flynn had tried to get up and follow, intending to help. He hadn't made it far—Huck had found him passed out on the floor beside the bed. He'd only recently regained consciousness. Huck was hoping for information that could lead him to Lonaker, and now he felt like he was on the verge of getting it.

"If they wore hoods, how could you know?"

"Their voices. I recognized the voices of two of them. One was Simon Dockery. He runs a general store here in town. The other was Billy Endicott. A local boy. One of Miss Kincade's pupils. Dockery seemed to be the man in charge. Which doesn't surprise me. He ordered one of his men to finish me off. That's when Lonaker stepped in and offered to do the job. Insisted on it. I tell you, I wasn't thinking too many nice things about your friend right then. I was wrong about him."

"Only when the dog was drowning did anyone offer him a drink," murmured Huck.

"What?"

"Nothing. Lonaker's a hard man to figure out. A hard man to like."

"I wish I could help you find him," growled Flynn, frustrated by his helplessness. "I owe him that much. To think, we were on the same side all along."

"No idea where they might have taken him?"

"Up into the mountains, be my guess. But exactly where? I don't have a clue. The Big Marias cover a lot of country, and they're still plenty wild. A few lumber camps, a mine or two, and that's about it. Plenty of places to hide."

"Bet this Dockery fella would know."

"What makes you think you could get anything out of him? He'll be as tight-lipped as that man Howell we've got locked up in the jail. These damned secesh are fanatics."

"All I can do is try."

"Just watch your back. God only knows how many of our fine citizens are actually Copperheads. They hide like snakes in tall grass. You don't know they're there until one of them bites you. It's a bad business, this rebellion. You don't know who to trust. You can't tell what side a man is on unless he's got the guts to stand up and tell you to your face. Seems to me most of these rebel heroes don't have the guts. They'd rather shoot you in the back."

"Where is Dockery's store?"

"Next street over. Go back through the alley and take a right turn. You'll come to it. He's a widower—lives alone in a room in the back of the store. But I don't know if he'll be there."

"One way to find out."

"Get one of the men at the jail to go with you."

"And how do you know you can trust either one of them, Sheriff?"

Flynn scowled, because he knew he couldn't.

Huck took his leave. In the outer office, Mobley was sprawled in a maroon leather wing chair, sound asleep, spectacles almost sliding off his nose, a medical journal about to slide off his knees. Huck gently lifted the journal and saw the pistol on Mobley's lap. The reinsman shook his head and laid the journal on the desk. It was a sorry state of affairs when a man who had committed his life to saving the lives of others had to concern himself with protecting his patients from assassins.

Huck tiptoed out and down the staircase. Flynn's warning in mind, he warily searched the night shadows as he proceeded down the alley to the next street over. He soon found Dockery's general store. The shebang was closed up tight. No lights in the windows. He pounded on the door with his big fist, hard enough to shake the entire building, and got no response. Disappointed, he headed on up the street toward the riverfront, where the hotel was located, intending to check on Sancho and find out from Miss Kincade where Billy Endicott could be found. He walked fast.

Something told him Lonaker was running out of time.

Chapter Twenty-seven

Lonaker figured they would be after him plenty pronto. He'd cut the head off the snake by killing Lightfoot, but that alone wasn't going to stop the secessionists. Dockery was still alive, and so was Homer Raney. Both were born leaders. This snake was still dangerous.

After running as fast as he dared along the ledge for a few hundred yards, he stopped to catch his breath, and found a place to make a stand. He decided it would be to his advantage to catch his pursuers here, where the ledge was particularly narrow and jacklegged around a stone abutment which provided him with some cover. They couldn't get around him — on one side was a sheer drop into Sidewinder Gorge, and on the other a sheer cliff loomed high overhead. They would have to go through him, and do so one at a time. Reloading the Colt revolvers, he waited.

And waited.

After a half-hour of waiting he started having second thoughts. Maybe he'd thrown the rebels into such confusion that the pursuit had been delayed. Perhaps no one had stepped forward to lead them. Dockery was on his way back to Seven Springs, unaware of what had transpired, and it was possible that Raney was still unconscious.

And even if they did eventually organize pursuit, how fast could they move, taking the ledge on horseback in the dark?

Lonaker changed his mind and started moving again. Even afoot he could make fairly good time on the ledge. No sense in hanging around all night waiting for them to catch up. His best hope was to cover as much ground as possible before dawn. The night was his ally.

His destination was Seven Springs. He had no other choice. He needed a fast horse to get him to Fort Yuma. He couldn't count on Huck being in town—he had no way of knowing where Huck was at this moment.

If he could deliver the list of Golden Circle members to Colonel Dahlgren, maybe the Army would be inclined to listen when he tried to explain about the payroll.

He'd buried the payroll less than a mile from the Painted Rock station. He couldn't spare the time to detour that far to retrieve it before heading for Fort Yuma. His first priority had to be getting the list of names to the Army.

Assuming, of course, that he got out of the Big Marias alive.

He made it off the ledge without mishap. Having paid careful attention to the route Dockery had choen bringing him to the Copperhead camp, he had no trouble backtracking, despite the fact that he was unfamiliar with these mountains. The waning moon was just a sliver of silver in the night sky, but he could see well enough to stay his course.

Now he had to watch more than his backtrail. Simon Dockery was somewhere up ahead. The storekeeper couldn't have made it back to Seven Springs yet, and Lonaker thought it likely he would night in the mountains and arrive in town early next morning. Dockery had himself said that he'd established the routine of returning to Seven Springs on Sunday morning, in time for church. He would not break the routine.

When he saw the distant yellow glow of a campfire, the Overland troubleshooter knew it had to be Dockery's. Lonaker covered the intervening ground silent as a shadow. Day or night, he could move through brush without making a sound.

More than anything else it was Dockery's horse he was after. It wasn't in Lonaker to slip up on the storekeeper and shoot him down in cold blood. That was the kind of ruthless practicality Apaches employed. In this case Lonaker was almost sorry he didn't have the makings of a bushwhacker.

All he could do was try to get the jump on Dockery, disarm him and borrow the man's cayuse. It would slow him down too much to take Dockery along. Two men and one horse did not make for fast travel, and Lonaker knew that fast travel was the secret to his staying alive.

When he got close to the camp, Lonaker realized it

wasn't going to be easy to Indian-up on Dockery. The storekeeper had chosen a good place to pass the night. A clump of boulders lined the foot of a steep shale slope spotted with bristlecone pines. Dockery sat with his back to a boulder with a hundred feet of open ground, a shelf of blistered rock, in front of him. Lonaker would have to cover that open ground to reach the camp. The only other option was to circle up onto the slope and try to slip down behind Dockery, but chances were better than good that the loose shale would give him away.

Worse still, Dockery was keeping his horse close, the reins tied to a rock the size and weight of a blacksmith's anvil.

Lonaker got in as close as he could, finding concealment in a clump of scrub juniper on the rim of the shelf. While he pondered the problem of getting closer, he heard horses. He slipped deeper into the juniper and lay flat on his belly. Seven riders passed within a stone's throw of his hiding place. He could see them clearly. Raney was in the lead. The edge of the dressing around his head showed beneath his hat.

Lonaker had finally caught up with him.

They moved in on Dockery's camp with guns drawn. From where he lay, Lonaker could see Dockery fade back into the rocks, rifle in hand. But when Raney and the others rode into the firelight, Dockery emerged.

"What are you doing here, Raney?" asked the storekeeper. "What happened?"

"It's Lonaker. He killed Captain Lightfoot. Got away with the list of society members."

"Lightfoot and his damned list," said Dockery, disgusted.

"We were hoping this might be Lonaker's camp," said one of the riders.

"John Lonaker is no fool," said Raney.

"No," said Dockery. "But he made a fool of us, didn't he? Sure fooled me. He killed Flynn — how could that be?"

Lonaker could hear every word. He was too close for comfort, but he didn't dare move now. Dockery sounded very calm. A little stunned, but no anger, no panic. And no question that the others looked to him for leadership. He was Lightfoot's heir apparent, a man who remained cool and collected in a crisis.

There was a moment of silence, as desperate men thought desperate thoughts.

"He was on foot," said Raney, finally. "He can't get far tonight. He can't get out of these mountains before tomorrow."

Dockery put another piece of wood on the fire. Sitting on his heels, he stared into the flames. The others remained mounted, waiting for his decision.

"He'll try to get to Fort Yuma, deliver that list to the army," decided Dockery. "But he needs a horse, and the only place for him to get one is Seven Springs. One of you men must ride into town. Who knows Billy Endicott, Frank Johnson or Joe Fraley?"

"I know Fraley," replied one of the horsemen. "He's clerk at the Riverfront Hotel, ain't he?"

Dockery nodded. "He boards there, too. That's where you'll find him. Ride in and tell him what happened. I want every member of the society in Seven

Springs on the lookout for John Lonaker tomorrow, spread out all over town and ready to shoot to kill. The rest of you will ride with me. We'll watch the valley. Try to catch him out in the open before he ever gets to Seven Springs. He's got to be stopped."

"That means all our men in town will have to lay their cards on the table," said Raney. "Everyone will know what they are and what they're up to."

"Everyone will know anyway, if Lonaker gets that list to the Army."

"What if he doesn't go into Seven Springs at all?" asked Raney, playing devil's advocate.

Dockery stood up and slowly scanned the night. He looked right at Lonaker's hiding place. Then his steely gaze moved on.

"What's he going to do? He can't strike out due south. It would take him days to walk around Sidewinder Gorge, and days more to walk across the desert to Yuma, even if he could make such a trip on foot. And we could waste days searching these mountains, and not find a man who doesn't want to be found. No more sneaking around, hiding under hoods, boys. It's time to start the war. And the first order of business is to kill John Lonaker."

The man who claimed to know Fraley rode off into the darkness. The others dismounted. They loosened cinches but did not unsaddle their horses. They spread their blankets on the ground, and while the others stretched out to catch some sleep, Raney and Dockery sat around the fire awhile, talking in low tones.

Lonaker could hear little of what they were saying

He lay there in the juniper, within spitting distance of seven men who meant to kill him first chance they got, and considered his options. He didn't have many. Dockery was right. He needed a horse. These men kept theirs close even while they slept. No chance to steal one out of this camp. So his only other choice was Seven Springs. But how could he get into and out of town unseen?

After an hour of cussing and discussing, Dockery and Raney turned in. The fire had died down to a bed of orange embers. Lonaker waited a while longer and then crawled out of the juniper and slipped away from the sleeping camp.

By the time the first pink and orange shades of dawn began to color the eastern sky, Lonaker was on the road twisting like a snake down the wooded flank of the Big Marias and out into the valley. He chose to keep to the road as long as possible, although he figured Dockery and the others were already on the move and would use this very road to reach the sagebrush flats west of Seven Springs.

A half-hour later, when he heard horses, he sought cover in the timber. But it wasn't Dockery's bunch. It was the old-timer he'd met day before yesterday just outside Seven Springs, driving the same old rickety supply wagon.

As the wagon rolled near, Lonaker drew one of his Colt Dragoons and stepped out of the brush. The codger hauled back on the reins and stopped his mules.

"Hoss, if this hyar's a holdup," rasped the old-timer, "you'd best find yoreself another line of work, 'cause you ain't got the sense God gave chickens. This hyar wagon's as empty as my pockets."

"I need a ride into town," said Lonaker.

The gristleneck peered at the troubleshooter's pistol with a jaundiced eye. "Wahl, you got a funny way of askin' for it."

"I need to know something first," replied Lonaker. "Tell me how you feel about secession."

Chapter Twenty-eight

The old-timer grinned ear-to-ear. It pleased him no end when someone asked him how he felt about this or what he thought about that. He was always willing to pontificate on a subject, and he tended to be long-winded. It didn't matter if he really knew what he was talking about, or had any experience in the matter.

Settling back on the wagon seat, he fished a block of Lobo Negro chewing tobacco from the pocket of his blanket coat and tore off a chunk with crooked yellow teeth. He chewed a moment, looking skyward, collecting his thoughts.

"Well?" rasped Lonaker, who didn't have all day.

"Way I see it," said the old-timer, "this hyar United States was thrown together with the notion that the majority's supposed to rule. Seein' as how you can't please ever'body all the time, that makes sense to me. This way, what's best for the mostest people is what gets done. Now, if a feller has an idea that's good for him and mebbe a handful of others, but ain't no good for most folks, he's got to figure out some other way to get ahead that ain't so bad for so many people."

Lonaker sighed. "What does this have to do with secession?"

The old gristleneck scowled at Lonaker. "I'm gettin' around to it."

"If you were trying for Santa Fe I guess you'd go by way of China," said the troubleshooter.

The old-timer haughtily refused to grace this snide comment with a retort.

"That's the problem with these secesh," he continued. "They ain't willin' to abide by the will of the majority. Instead of tryin' to compromise and live with other folks, they don't bother thinkin' about nobody but themselves. Iffen we was to let ever'body have their way, why we wouldn't have no country at all. Folks'd be goin' around shootin' holes in ever'body who disagreed with them about every little ol' thing. Want my opinion?"

Lonaker grimaced.

The old-timer didn't wait for more of the troubleshooter's sarcasm. "My opinion, we got to teach these rebels a thing or two about democracy. They've got freedom and democracy mixed up. Freedom don't mean you can go around doin' any ol' thing you wanna do, with no never mind about it hurtin' other folks. You got the freedom to do what you want only so long as it don't muddy somebody else's water.

"Now these damned slaveholders got their hackles up, and they've got a lot of other folks who don't have nothin' to do with slavery all up in arms because they're talkin' up freedom like it's the glue what holds a democracy together. I find that kinda funny—these fancy-rich gentlemen yellin' about freedom when they got slaves they don't treat much better than livestock."

Lonaker had holstered the Colt revolvers by this time. "That answers my question," he said wryly. "I think. Like I said, I need a ride into town. But you ought to know, I've got some of those rebels on my trail." He glanced up the road, listening hard. What he heard made his heart pump faster. "In fact, I reckon that's them now."

"Slide on back into them trees and sit tight," said the old-timer.

Lonaker did as he was told. He didn't have much choice. Either the old-timer gave him away or he didn't. He wasn't sure if he trusted the codger. The man sounded sincere enough, but recent experience had left the Overland troubleshooter wondering if he would ever be capable of trusting anyone again.

Dockery, Raney and their five associates came down the road in a big hurry. The old-timer watched them with a calm, untroubled demeanor. They checked their lathered horses and circled the supply wagon.

"We're looking for a man," said Dockery. "A man on foot, wearing a buckskin jacket and carrying a matched pair of ivory-handled pistols."

"What fur?" queried the old-timer.

Unprepared for the question, Dockery glanced at Raney.

"He's an outlaw," said the quick-thinking Raney. "Wanted for murder and robbery. Stole an Army payroll. A real desperate character, friend. I work for the Overland Mail Company. This is Simon Dockery. He runs a general store in Seven Springs."

"I know Mr. Dockery. He knows me. I buy supplies from him and haul 'em up to the lumber camp. That's what I do. Haul supplies. And mind my own business."

Dockery's smile was thin. He leaned forward in his saddle, and there was a subtle menace in that move, as well as in his quiet voice.

"You saying you wouldn't tell us if you'd seen this man?"

The old-timer glanced at the other five riders and knew them for what they were: hard-cases, who would have no qualms about filling him full of lead just for the hell of it.

"I ain't got to be this long in the tooth by being a damfool. Seein' as how I mind my own business, like I said, it don't really matter to me what you're after this feller for."

"Then why did you ask?" snapped Dockery.

"Bad habit. I ain't seen nobody since I left the lumber camp, except you boys."

Dockery glanced into the wagon bed, empty but for a folded canvas tarp used to cover the supplies in case of inclement weather. He did know the old-timer, and concluded that there was nothing out of the ordinary about his being on this road on this particular morning. He nodded and turned to Raney.

"Lonaker wouldn't be foolish enough to stick to the road anyway. Besides, he probably hasn't gotten this far yet. Let's go on down to the valley. We might get lucky and catch him out in the open."

They rode on. Lonaker waited until they were out of sight before breaking cover.

"You steal an Army payroll, hoss?" asked the old-timer.

"Yes. But I intend to give it back. I needed it to convince those men to trust me long enough for me to get this."

He pulled the oilskin-wrapped portfolio from beneath his shirt. He didn't waste time explaining that it had been one man's identity that he'd been after, and that acquiring the roster of the Golden Circle society had just been good fortune.

"What's that?" asked the old-timer.

Lonaker told him.

The oldtimer spat tobacco juice between the haunches of the rearmost pair of hard-tails in the hitch.

"Those scoundrels are lower than a snake's belly, in my book. Climb in back, partner. Crawl up under that thar tarp and I'll get you to town, come hell, high water, or rebels."

Chapter Twenty-nine

Lonaker heard church bells as the wagon rolled into Seven Springs. He couldn't see anything though, being completely covered by the canvas tarp and lying flat in the bed of the wagon. Aware that the local chapter of the Golden Circle was by now on the alert and watching for him, he asked the old-timer to be his eyes.

"Bunch of folks dressed up to the nines and headin' for church," replied the old-timer, talking out of the side of his mouth and being careful not to turn his head. "Wait just a doggone minute. Sumpin else. I see men standin' around here and there, now that I look closer. Thar's one over by the barber shop. Another in the alley yonder. A third sittin' on a bench in front of the gunsmith's shop. They're trying mighty hard to look casual, but these are sharp-eyed pilgrims."

"They're looking for me," said Lonaker. "They're secessionists."

He heard the old-timer hawk and spit.

"That's what I think of them and their cause," declared the old-timer, belligerently.

As prearranged, he steered the wagon to the local livery, which Lonaker had decided was the place to get a horse.

The big double doors of the livery were open, and the old-timer drove the wagon straight into the carriageway. He pulled hard on the leathers to stop his mules.

"Wah!, I'll be . . ." he muttered, awestruck.

"What's wrong?" hissed Lonaker.

"Nothin's wrong. Just the first time I seen an honest-to-God stagecoach in Seven Springs."

"Stagecoach!"

Lonaker threw the tarp aside and stood up in the bed of the wagon. He was relieved to be out from under the heavy canvas, and even more relieved to see Betsy. His custom-made Concord, with six-horse hitch rigged and ready, almost filled the carriageway.

And there stood Huck, bullwhip coiled and hanging on his shoulder, as usual. Lonaker had never been so happy to see anyone in his entire life.

"Been expecting you, Mr. Lonaker," said Huck. "We're ready to roll. If you want my opinion, the sooner we get out of this town the better. Place is crawling with rebels."

Lonaker jumped down out of the wagon. "I see Sancho found you."

"He did better than that. He came with me.

Only we tangled with a couple of no-account bounty hunters who were after your scalp. He took a bullet, but he'll be all right. He's laid up in the hotel down by the river. I figure he's safer there than with us, today."

"That's a guaranteed fact," nodded Lonaker. "I've got to get to Fort Yuma, Huck."

"Colonel Dahlgren will be glad to see you—if you've got the Army's money."

"I don't. It's buried, not a mile from Painted Rock. I've got something worth ten payrolls. A list of the names of all the Knights of the Golden Circle."

"So I heard."

"Where did you hear that? And how did you know I was coming?"

"I was at the hotel last night, checking on Sancho. As I was walking down the hall I heard two men talking in one of the rooms. Now, I don't make a habit of eavesdropping, mind you, but one of them happened to mention your name as I went by, so I stopped and listened at the door. One man was saying you had killed a Captain Lightfoot and gotten away with that list. He said Dockery had figured you would be coming here, and that they were supposed to keep their eyes peeled, and how you had to be stopped. I decided the best thing for me to do was to get Betsy ready to roll and sit tight. Been here since before first light."

"I'm glad you're here, Huck."

"I just wish you'd told me what you were up to from the get-go."

"I couldn't do that." Lonaker turned to the old-timer and extended his hand. The latter was still perched on the wagon seat, methodically chewing his tobacco.

"Thanks for your help," said the troubleshooter.

"Don't mention it. Least I could do."

Lonaker glanced through the open doors at the stretch of sun-hammered street beyond. The church bells had stopped ringing. Most of Seven Springs' decent, law-abiding folks were safely tucked away by now, getting this week's dose of fire and brimstone. Real hell, he mused, was about to break loose.

And then he thought of Molly Kincade—wondered if he would see her again, and wished he could see her now.

"There's a young lady in town," said Huck, as though he were reading Lonaker's mind, "who seems to think highly of you, Mr. Lonaker. Too bad we don't have time to stop by the hotel and see her. She's watching over Sancho, taking care of him. Real nice lady."

"Maybe tomorrow," said Lonaker gruffly. "If we see tomorrow."

" 'To live in hearts we leave behind is not to die,' " quote Huck. "Campbell."

Lonaker grinned at the reinsman. "Some things never change. Let's roll."

He climbed into the coach, opened the guncase,

211

and took out the Remington ten-gauge and a box of shells. These he passed through the sliding panel above the forward seat to Huck, who had clambered up into the box.

"Take it nice and easy at first," cautioned the troubleshooter. "Maybe they'll be slow in figuring it out."

He closed and secured the hickory shutters over the windows and threw open the roof hatch. As Huck whipped up the team, Lonaker reached for the Sharps buffalo gun and wished he still had the Henry repeater.

Huck nodded at the old-timer as the stagecoach rolled past the wagon, and the old-timer gave the thumbs-up sign. Working the leathers with hands and wrists of agile steel, the reinsman turned the Concord up the street, holding the six-horse-hitch at something less than road gait.

A man stepped out of boardwalk shade as the coach neared his position. He had his hand resting on the pistol in his belt. He glared at Huck, and Huck nodded with a pleasant smile. The man's suspicious eyes raked the near-side of the Concord. He started walking after it, looking around for a sign from one of his cohorts.

The street was virtually empty. The stores were closed, and most folks were in church. Above the drumming of hooves and the rattle of the coach, Huck heard the churchgoers singing a hymn — a pleasant sound, but also, under the circumstances, somewhat incongruous.

Rebels were coming out of the woodwork now, on both sides of the street. Huck counted five in front of him—three on his left, two on his right. He didn't know how many were in the street behind him. At least one, probably more. He didn't turn to look; instead, he watched the five men fan out directly in the path of the Concord.

"Five in front," he said.

Lonaker was looking through the sliding panel. "I see them. Keep going."

One of the rebels was Billy Endicott. Another Lonaker recognized as the man named Johnson. The troubleshooter wondered if he and Huck could bluff their way through. He didn't like hiding from these men—it cut against his grain. But once they saw him the killing would start. And Lonaker thought it would be nice to get out of this without more killing. A forlorn hope, he knew. But hope sprang eternal. Alexander Pope, wasn't it?

As it became apparent to them that Huck wasn't going to stop the coach just because they were standing in the way, the five secessionists exchanged glances. Three drew their pistols. One of these was Billy Endicott, who surged forward and waved his gun in a menacing fashion at Huck.

"You, stop! Stop, you hear me?"

Huck had plenty of nerve. He smiled, saluted, and kept going. Billy trotted alongside, brandishing the pistol. The pistol distracted Huck. He didn't see Johnson dart toward the coach on the off-side. Johnson grabbed the door and wrenched it open. The first thing he saw was Lonaker. The last thing was the troubleshooter's Colt spitting flame. The impact of the bullet at such close range hurled Johnson ten feet.

Then everybody started shooting.

Chapter Thirty

One of the rebels was a quick thinker. He shot the off-side leader. The horse dropped in its traces, throwing the rest of the team into a panic. The dead horse acted like an anchor, bringing the stagecoach to a standstill.

Billy Endicott fired at Huck, and missed. Huck dropped the reins and ducked down into the front boot. Another secessionist blasted away at the boot, thinking all he had to shoot through was leather. His bullets tore through the leather, but could not penetrate the hickory and oak panels beneath. Huck popped up with the Remington shotgun and emptied one barrel of double-ought into the rebel. He swung the ten-gauge in Billy Endicott's direction and pulled the trigger. But Billy was quick. He rolled under the Concord. The buckshot kicked up street dust, missing Endicott cleanly.

Huck dropped down into the boot again as the other two rebels started shooting. Hot lead splintered the Concord. Huck flinched—he could almost feel every bullet ripping into his beloved Betsy.

Lonaker fired through the sliding panel and brought one Copperhead down. The other ran for cover, shooting wildly over his shoulder until his pistol dry-fired. Lonaker, standing on the bench seat, could get his head and shoulders through the roof hatch. At the same time, Huck rose from the front boot, snapping the reloaded Remington shut. The rebel was running for his life now, throwing away his empty gun.

"Let him go," said Lonaker.

Huck grinned. "There's hope for you yet."

Bullets burned the air. Lonaker glimpsed four more secessionists closing in from behind them as he dropped down into the coach. Huck's shotgun roared again. One of the secessionists dropped, clutching a leg shredded by buckshot. The rest scattered, seeking cover, one to the corner of a building, a second belly-down behind a water trough, the third kneeling behind a barrel on the boardwalk in front of a dry goods store. They began plugging away at the Concord.

Lonaker figured it was time to introduce the Sharps buffalo gun. Again standing on the bench-seat, he thrust his head and shoulders through the roof hatch and steadied the long barrel of the rifle on the top rack's railing. The "Old Poison Slinger" had an effective killing range of over a mile. Lonaker's first shot went right through the barrel behind which one of the Copperheads was crouching, and through the man behind it.

Throwing the trigger guard forward dropped a sliding block to expose the buffalo gun's breech.

The troubleshooter inserted another linen cartridge and drew the trigger guard back into place. The rising block sheared off the top of the cartridge, exposing the charge. Lonaker peered through the Sharps' leaf sight and drew a bead on the man behind the water trough. The rifle boomed once more. The slug pierced the trough and killed the man behind it.

And then, just when Lonaker was beginning to think he had the battle won, seven riders came charging down the street with guns blazing.

It was Dockery, Raney and their bunch, drawn by the sound of gunfire.

The men who rode with Dockery and Raney had all spent some time on the owlhoot trail. They'd lived by the gun, and knew how to shoot. A hail of bullets pounded the Concord. Lonaker was trying to reload the Sharps when a bullet struck the buffalo gun and knocked it out of his grasp. Another slug whined off the top rack rail. A third hit Lonaker high in the shoulder. Stunned, he dropped down into the coach. He fumbled with the Colt Dragoons, shouted hoarsely above the gun thunder at Huck, telling the reinsman to keep his head down. Huck yelled back, but Lonaker couldn't make out the words above the din of galloping horses and the crash of gunfire. The shooting seemed to be coming from both ends of the street now. Lonaker's heart sank. There were even more Copperheads than he'd thought. The odds were too heavy, after all. His luck had run out.

All he could do was go out fighting.

217

Steeling himself, he burst out of the stagecoach, a Colt in either hand.

At that moment, a dozen troopers galloped past. Lonaker threw himself against the side of the coach to avoid being trampled. He watched in amazement as the cavalrymen swept past. More had appeared behind Dockery and his rebels. Colonel Dahlgren was leading the charge, waving his saber high overhead with one hand, firing his pistol with the other, the reins in his teeth.

Caught in a crossfire, the Copperheads had no chance. Men fell on both sides. Horses, too. Through the dust and gunsmoke, Lonaker saw Raney fall. Dahlgren's saber flashed in the hot sunlight and Simon Dockery fell, fighting to the last breath.

Abruptly, the shooting stopped.

"Lonaker!"

The troubleshooter turned, saw Molly Kincade running down the street from the hotel. He took a few unsteady steps, whirled as Huck yelled a warning.

On his belly beneath the Concord, Billy Endicott fired. The bullet struck Lonaker in the side, knocking him to the ground. As he fell he triggered both Colts, a reflex action. Flat on his back, he tried to lift the pistols, but they were too heavy to lift. He was vaguely aware that Endicott wasn't shooting any more. Had he gotten Billy? He really didn't care. It didn't seem to matter. He was too tired . . .

"John."

He forced his eyes open. As though through a

red haze, he saw Huck bending over him. Then he saw Molly, felt the cool, soft touch of her hand in his, and passed out with a smile on his face.

When he came to, her hand was still in his, and at first he thought he'd only been out for a moment — before he realized he was lying in a bed instead of the street. The counterpane and sheet were pulled up and tucked under his arms. The dressing around his chest and shoulder was very tight, constricting his breathing.

But at least I'm breathing.

He opened his eyes, blinked away the mist, and found himself in a small room, big enough for the bed he lay in, the chair she was sitting in pulled up close beside the bed, and a chest of drawers crowned by a cheap mirror. Dust motes danced in a shaft of sunlight slanting through the window. He watched them dance a moment, trying to remember what had happened.

"Thank God in heaven," breathed Molly when his eyes flickered open.

She squeezed his hand and he smiled at her.

"I was hoping I'd see you again," he said. He felt it needed saying, although talking was difficult for him. His tongue seemed swollen to twice its normal size, and his throat was as dry as the dust in a dead man's pockets.

"I'm just damned glad you're alive," said Colonel Dahlgren, looming behind Molly's chair. "Since you're the only one who knows where the payroll is."

"List," croaked Lonaker. "Did you get the list?"

Dahlgren held the portfolio up. Lonaker saw the bullet hole in it, the bloodstains. His blood. He remembered now.

"You mean this?" asked the Colonel. "Mr. Odom explained it all to me. By God, Lonaker, you had a lot of gall, risking the Army's money in such a harebrained scheme. I don't know how you pulled it off, frankly. You couldn't again in a million years."

"But it was worth it, wasn't it, Colonel?" asked Molly, leaping to Lonaker's defense.

Dahlgren looked at her, at the list, and then at Lonaker. A slow grin pulled apart the scowl on his hawkish features.

"Yes, it was. We're going to put every last one of these traitors behind bars. Isn't that right, Sergeant?"

Macready stepped into Lonaker's line of sight and took the portfolio Dahlgren was holding out to him.

"Aye, sir. Flamin' rabble. I just hope a few of the beggars put up a fight. A better fight than the one we had yesterday."

"Yesterday?" echoed Lonaker.

"You'll get your fight," promised Dahlgren, the grin making way for a grimace. "Before this war is over, Macready, even you might have your fill of fighting."

Macready seemed to take offense to this suggestion. He drew himself up, stiff with indignation.

"Not I, sir!" he vociferated.

Dahlgren turned to Lonaker. "I'll leave a detail behind. When you can ride, I'd appreciate it if you would lead them to the payroll. My men would very much like to be paid."

Lonaker nodded. The Colonel turned to go, took a step, glanced back at the Overland trouble-shooter.

"You may have singlehandedly saved California for the Union, Mr. Lonaker. And, for what it's worth, you've almost restored my faith in civilians."

As soon as Dahlgren and the Irish three-striper had gone, Lonaker said, "Molly, I . . ."

"Yes?"

He lost his courage. "Where am I?"

"The hotel. Sancho is in the next room. The owner, Mr. Wingate, says he's thinking about turn-ing this place into a hospital."

It was a joke, but Lonaker took it seriously. "We'll need a lot more hospitals before this thing is over."

There came a knock on the door. It was Huck, as always carrying his bullwhip. Seeing Lonaker conscious was a big relief to the ex-prizefighter.

"I knew you'd make it, Mr. Lonaker."

"Huck, isn't it about time you started calling me John?"

Huck was deeply moved. "Thanks . . . John." He was suddenly solemn. "I just got word from the Yuma station. An urgent message came down the line for you, from Mr. Fargo himself." Reluctant to go on, he scratched his head and shifted weight from one leg to the other self-consciously.

"That bad?" asked Lonaker. "Don't tell me they put a price on my head."

"Well, Phil Coffman already did that. But that'll be taken care of."

"What is it, then?"

"They've decided to shut down the Oxbow Route."

Lonaker just stared, thunderstruck.

Huck nodded. "With Texas gone over to the Confederacy, they figure the Oxbow can't be kept open. So they're moving the line north, lock, stock and barrel. The Pony Express route. Across the plains from St. Joseph, through South Pass and then across the Sierra Nevada to Sacramento."

Lonaker recalled that it was just what Homer Raney had suggested days ago, when they'd met at the Lime Creek station.

"Makes sense," said Lonaker, his voice growing stronger as he realized what a challenge the move would be. "That will be the way of the first railroad, too, in time."

A new line, across the prairie he knew so well.

"They want you to get started on the move right away," said Huck. "Of course, they don't know you're laid up like this. But they've put it all in your hands. It's a big job, Mr. Lonaker . . . I mean, John."

Lonaker looked at Molly. She was watching him, her eyes bright and intense, her lips parted slightly as she waited in breathless anticipation.

"I was just wondering," said Huck softly, "if we were going to do it."

Lonaker swallowed the lump in his throat. "I think I'm going to stay here, Huck."

She squeezed his hand again and smiled, even though it looked to Lonaker as though she was about to cry.

"But the Overland is your home," she said. "Don't they need schoolteachers on the plains?"

Laid up in bed with three bullet holes in him and barely able to breathe, John Lonaker had never felt better in his life.

"Well, you just take your time healing up," said Huck cheerily. "I've got a lot of work to do on poor old Betsy." He headed for the door.

"How many bullet holes now?" asked Lonaker.

"One hundred and forty-six," groaned the reinsman. "But Betsy's kind of like this country of ours. Nothing's going to stop her."

But Lonaker wasn't listening, because Molly had leaned over to kiss him.

Huck smiled. " 'All's well that ends well,' " he said as he stepped out of the room and gently shut the door behind him.